Mist and Vengeance

Sequel to Silent Twin

Tracy Plehn

Order this book online at www.trafford.com
or email orders@trafford.com

Most Trafford titles are also available at major online book retailers.

Print information available on the last page.

ISBN: 978-1-4907-8272-0 (sc)
ISBN: 978-1-4907-8274-4 (hc)
ISBN: 978-1-4907-8273-7 (e)

Library of Congress Control Number: 2017907842

Trafford rev. 05/19/2017

 www.trafford.com

North America & international
toll-free: 1 888 232 4444 (USA & Canada)
fax: 812 355 4082

Dedication

This is dedicated to my mom, without her support, encouragement and editing skills Mist and Vengeance would not have happened. Also, to all my friends and family for their support and patience through both books.

Contents

Contents

Chapter 1

All four of us finally arrived at our island resort in the Virgin Islands. After all we had been through, this was a much needed vacation. We settled in our rooms at the hotel; Jesse and I in one room and Cassie and Damien in the adjoining room. We decided to meet on the beach right outside our rooms in half an hour.

We found a spot without many people and spread our blankets on the white sand. The guys set up the umbrellas and snacks while Cassie and I ran to the beach bar to grab drinks for all of us.

We stood at the bar while waiting for our order of four cold beers. I turned to admire my guy from a distance. He and Damien were sitting on our blankets on the beach. Jesse stared at me as Damien talked his ear off. After a few minutes of gazing at each other from a distance, he stood up and took off his shirt. He knew that would drive me crazy, taunting me with that gorgeous tanned and muscular body... I couldn't take my eyes off him!

He is so cute! I heard a chuckle in my head! *Wait, did he heard me?!*

"Jesse get out of my head!"

"Quit making it so easy brat!" He laughed in his head so I could hear him. Suddenly the bantering turned to something else. I saw his eyes turn that weird red color and his gaze went to my left.

I looked in the same direction but didn't see anything. I turned back to him but he was gone! I glanced a few feet from where he stood then back to the blanket where Damien had been sitting, the blanket was empty. I looked back and forth between the water and blanket. Nothing! People walked past, played in the water and built their sand castles as if life was normal and two grown men hadn't just disappeared! What was wrong with them?!

Ok, calm down. They must have gone into the water.

"You guys can't stay under forever you know! It's not funny Jesse! Answer me!" Neither of them responded to my thoughts. There was just silence.

"Mandy, what's wrong?" Cassie must have noticed how nervous I was.

"I can't find the guys. I looked away from them for a second and now they're gone. Jesse was being goofy then his eyes...his eyes glowed! He looked over there but I couldn't see what he saw." Cassie paid for the drinks but we left them on the bar and ran down to the beach to look for them. We split up and walked in opposite directions hollering for them.

I stood at the edge of the water and looked up and down the beach. Did they go back to the hotel? No, they would've told us. It didn't make sense. I saw Cassie walking toward me about fifty feet up the beach. I was going to tell her to check the room but Jesse started *speaking* to me. I dropped to my knees in the sand...

"Mandy!! Can you hear me?! I don't know what the hell is happening! We're above you, I can see you but I think we're too high for you to see us! Damien and I have been taken by...by a...um, I don't know what. Something huge grabbed us! Oh no, I can't see you! Mandy can you hear me?! If you can, then both of you get back home and wait for us! Somehow..."

"Wait, what? 'Somehow' what?! Jesse where are you?! I didn't understand what you said! JESSE!!" I was gripping the sides of my head trying to hear him but he was gone. I'm not sure how long I had been in this position. I stood up almost falling over but Cassie grabbed me. I was dizzy. I looked around, the people that had been enjoying their fun beach day stopped to stare at the crazy lady in the sand.

"Mandy! Are you okay? What just happened?!"

"I don't know. Jesse was talking to me, in my head! He said they were grabbed by something huge and it was taking them higher and higher. The last thing he said was for us to go back home and wait for them." I regained my composure and took Cassie by the arm to guide her toward the hotel.

"He can forget about that! I'm not leaving until we find them!" I ranted as we ran back to the room.

"Mandy, I don't understand. How did they just disappear? Where did they go? What took them?" Cassie was stumbling to keep up with me so I slowed down.

"I'm sorry Cassie. I didn't mean to grab you like that but we have to get back to the room and try to figure out our next step. I don't have an answer to any of your questions right now." She was still recovering physically and mentally from her kidnapping and for a second I had forgotten that. I needed to be careful with her. As we walked to the hotel I wanted to try and 'reach' Jesse. I knew it would be futile but I didn't know what else to do. Mine and Jesse's internal cell service was suddenly out of service but I had to try.

"Jesse, JESSE! Can you hear me?!" Nothing.

When we arrived at my room Cassie sat on the bed.

"How could this happen? All the bad stuff was supposed to be over! We were on vacation!" Cassie was very upset and tried holding in the tears.

"We'll figure it out, I promise. I'm sorry I got so crazy down there. I still don't understand these powers or whatever it is the guys have but they will find their way back to us. In the meantime, I want to figure out what happened to them." I sat on the bed next to her and try to console her. I really need to remember how fragile she is.

She wriggled out of my grasp and stood up.

"Mandy, let's go to my room. I think Damien's journals are in his suitcase, maybe there's a clue as to what happened. Maybe this has something to do with that island he was on."

"That's an awesome idea! Let's go!"

We got back to Cassie's room and she grabbed Damien's suitcase.

I found his journals and pulled them out of the bag.

"There has to be a clue somewhere." I was frantic and my mind raced in 500 different directions.

"Mandy, do you think they're still...that they are okay?"

"Cassie, stop it! Of course they're okay and we're going to find them! I think whatever happened to Damien on that island has everything to do with this." Damien had told Jesse about the experiences he had on the island but had not shared much of the information with me. I started plowing through the pages of his journals for any kind of clue.

After searching for an hour, I took a break and called home. I spoke with Becca, my office manager, and filled her in with the details I thought she should know. I told her we would be delayed and to have my neighbor take over my students' riding lessons until I get back.

My neighbor and I would help each other out so we weren't chained to the ranches all the time. She reassured me everything would be taken care of and not to worry. I tried to act casual but Becca knows me too well and I was sure she could sense the urgency and worry in my voice.

Cassie and I tried to stay calm and prayed the guys would show up with some exciting story during the night. I continued thumbing through Damien's journals for awhile but there was nothing I could see that would lead us to the guys.

"Cassie, do you know where Damien's place is in Vegas?" I asked as I kept reading.

"Yeah. I guess we could go to his place but I'm sure that slime ball, TJ, has already ripped his place apart before he kidnapped me."

"Would you mind calling the airline and change our flight? If the guys don't show up tonight let's leave tomorrow for Vegas." She nodded and pulled out her cell phone.

I kept moving through the journals until we both passed out.

The next morning we woke early, the guys hadn't showed. We packed our bags and checked out at the front desk. The shuttle took us to the airport and we found our gate quickly after checking in the bags. We sat in the tan colored, hard plastic seats facing the window. It was hot and muggy in the airport. I wondered if the electric bill hadn't been paid and they shut off the air conditioning.

There was a family sitting to the right of Cassie and the little girl, maybe 7, was having a screaming fit. She was angry because her mother wouldn't give her some candy. Yep, that's what that child needed, sugar.

"Mandy?"

"Yeah?"

"I'm really scared. I don't know what to do next. What's going to happen?" Even though I was younger by two minutes, I had always been the "big sister". While growing up Cassie had been the impulsive one. She would never think before she jumped and I was usually the one to put her pieces back together. But looking at her now, she seemed frail and scared. I knew it would take a long time for her to recover from the horrible kidnapping ordeal. Now she has to deal with Damien disappearing. I wasn't sure how much more she could handle. I gave her a hug without saying a word.

They called our flight on the loudspeaker and we gathered our carry-on bags and stood in line to board.

Our plane had to make a stop in Puerto Rico for fuel and the pilot promised it would not be a long delay. The airstrip in Puerto Rico was extremely short and when the wheels hit the ground, the plane lurched forward and the engines whined. It didn't take long before we taxied back to the runway.

The flight to the Vegas airport was uneventful. We taxied to the gate and were informed we should stay seated until the plane came to a complete stop. Most obeyed, but a couple of people ignored the instructions and stood up to reclaim their belongings in the overhead compartment. They were in such a hurry to go nowhere fast. They had to stand and wait for the doors to open like the rest of us.

Cassie and I hadn't said a word to each other during the entire trip. We both stood and gathered our bags from the overhead bins and waited patiently for the line to move. We found our way to baggage claim, then to a rental car company. I didn't care what type of vehicle the company chose for us, but it turned out to be a nice one. It was a blue compact and still had the new car smell. The attendant went through the usual spiel, and we were on our way. I drove and Cassie navigated, since she knew the exact location of Damien's house.

We pulled into the driveway and it was not what I had expected. I'm not sure what I expected as I don't know Damien very well. Hmm, for that matter I haven't known Jesse very long, but he has become the love of my life. We had already been through a lifetime of challenges in these few short weeks. Our bond was intense. I felt his every emotion and he felt mine. We just had to find them.

The house was a red brick one-story ranch style with a covered front porch. It sat on a corner lot, with a large front and side yard. The driveway was cement and led to a two-car garage. I parked in front of the white garage door and got out. There was a big shade tree in front of the house and other than the lawn needing some attention, it was a very nice place.

"Do you have a key?" I hadn't thought of how we would get into the house until that very moment. Duh.

"No, but I know where he hides one." Cassie walked to the opposite side of the house furthest from the garage. There was a big barrel filled with potting soil for flowers. The copper strip around the barrel was loose in the back and Damien had taped a key to inside. Clever.

Cassie turned the key in the brass doorknob but didn't open it. She stood staring at it.

"Cassie, you okay?"

"I don't know. I just got a chill, like…we're being watched. I can't explain it but something's wrong." Her hand was trembling.

"Cassie, it's okay. I'm sure none of the kidnappers are alive. Remember, Jesse saw all of them in the hanger, dead." I gently took her hand away from the doorknob and turned it myself. I was anxious to see if there was anything that would lead us to the guys.

We entered the front door into the living room and stood side by side. We looked around. I could tell Damien was a neat freak. Unfortunately, TJ and his thugs had destroyed his once-tidy house. We stood on beautiful hardwood floors, to the right was a big bay window with a beige leather sofa and an oval oak coffee table. Those two pieces were still intact, but the matching end table lay on its side on the floor. On the other wall, next to the window, was a huge flat-screen television that I'm sure had been attached to the wall. It was in a thousand pieces on the floor.

I stepped a couple feet from the front door and rested my hands on a leather recliner that faced the TV wall. To the left of the chair, on the adjacent wall, was a red brick fireplace. All the knickknacks Damien had on the mantel were strewn all around the living room floor. The inside of the fireplace made a nasty, ashy mess throughout the room as well. These guys didn't miss a thing. Both Cassie and I stood frozen, looking around in disgust.

"Were they looking for Damien's journals?" I couldn't fathom what these journals could do for anyone but him.

"Yeah. He didn't get a chance to tell me much. He said if the journals got into TJ's or any of his thugs' hands, it would be really bad. Damien once trusted TJ. They grew up together, so Damien had no reason to think TJ would turn on him. But one day he 'accidentally' read TJ's mind. Good thing he did, because that gave him enough of a heads up to hide the journals." Cassie took a breath and sat on the sofa.

"I hope coming here wasn't a waste of time since we already have the journals with us. I didn't know TJ wanted them so badly. I didn't finish reading through them because I didn't understand a lot of the gibberish. Maybe further reading will prove helpful." I ran out the front door to the car and retrieved the journals from my duffel bag.

"Cassie, you go through the rest of the house and see if there's anything that may help us and I'll finish going through Damien's journals. Maybe he has something edible around this place, I'm starving."

I began rummaging through the first few pages from where I left off last night. There was still nothing I could make sense of – until I thumbed about a third of the way through one of them.

Damien finally started writing in laymen's terms. He described the island he had been living. I began to get my hopes up that somewhere in these pages would be the location of the island. Maybe they were taken back to that island. I knew it was a long shot but what else could I do? The little bit of information Jesse revealed to me gave me the impression that the island had 'changed' Damien somehow.

I looked up when I heard voices, then realized it was a television set, maybe in Damien's room. I paid no attention and continued reading...

> *"The chief has been very hospitable from the beginning... why? I'm an intruder on this island. I'm glad the tribe has taken me in, but it seems strange that they don't seem to question why I am here. I'm not even sure why I'm here myself. This wasn't my destination, but for some reason*

this island had a pull I couldn't resist. I have to write late at night when the tribe's asleep. I'm not sure they would like the idea of their secrets being on paper.

I've been here for thirteen days, and the language barrier is killing me. Sometimes they draw pictures in the dirt to help me understand what they're saying. I've gotten some of the basic words like food, drink, sleep, etc. but that's it so far. They seem to be as curious about me as I am about them. Their village is very primitive; huts made out of bamboo, and fire pits dug into the ground for cooking. There are 19 members of this tribe including the Chief. He and his wife, mate...not sure what they call themselves, have three sons. The second in command and his wife have one boy, and so on. Each of the 'mates' has at least one child.

One of the Chief's sons, maybe 14 years old, seems very leery of me. So far, he's the only one who has any reservations about my presence. That makes sense to me, but the others welcoming me so quickly is eerie. This boy watches me closely and I've tried putting him at ease, but he won't budge. He hasn't made a sound to me, just watches. I don't blame him a bit."

I was snapped out of my reading by Cassie's frantic voice. "Mandy! Mandy, come in here, quick!" I couldn't imagine what had happened, and hurried through the house, following the sound of the TV.

I got to the bedroom door, and there was Cassie, sitting on the four-poster king-size bed, watching TV.

"I wanted to get my mind off Damien so I thought I'd watch a sitcom or something, and this came on the news. Listen!" She turned up the volume to a newscast of some bizarre deaths that no one had been able to explain. It was a female reporter standing in the middle of a field. There was yellow police tape in a wide circle behind her.

"*Thank you, Steve. This is Sara Jackson reporting from a field outside of Red Rocks, Colorado. It's unbelievable! The police won't let us any closer than this, but from what we can tell so far, there are two people dead behind me. I have heard murmurs from officers and detectives that it could be the same killer who seemed to have started his rampage in Nevada. Their bodies seem to have imploded! I was able to sneak a glance and it was grisly and horrifying!*" The reporter paused as she wiped a tear from her eye, then continued.

"*It's just like the other 52 deaths! In the history of – well, the world – there has never been anything so terrible and unexplainable! There is no rhyme or reason to it, and they are so badly mutilated. Authorities are having a hard time identifying the victims.*" The camera panned back to the studio newscasters…

"*If you haven't been following this horrendous story, here's a brief recap. This began two months ago in the desert of Nevada, with the discovery of what they believe to be the first victim of the most bizarre and violent episode in history! The victims simply implode! Each body has been found in the middle of a field, an empty parking lot or an abandoned building. Their entire bodies explode from the inside out! The weirdness doesn't stop there, they found no explosives! So far, none of the bodies harbored any kind of explosive! It took weeks to identify the first victim but before they were able to figure out his identity, three more victims turned up in Nevada within two weeks.*

It didn't stop there…

There have been 52 victims so far, including today. The locations range from Nevada to California, Texas, Arizona and now Colorado. Officials haven't been able to give much detail in the case, as the investigation is still ongoing but I have to tell you that the concerns and fears among citizens in all these areas are overwhelming. Protestors have been outside the Capitol in Denver all afternoon demanding answers.

> *There is no apparent pattern. The victims range in age from 13 to 20; hair color varies; victims are both male and female; tall, medium, short stature; thin, large; no traceable pattern has been found as of yet, except they are young."*

Cassie turned off the television and turned to me. "What is going on, Mandy?"

"I don't know, Cassie – but I don't think this would have anything to do with Damien and Jesse, if that's what you're thinking." I knew this was scary news, but Cassie acted like this was the answer we were looking for. I couldn't quite figure out her thought process.

"I don't think it has to do with the guys. But I have this really creepy feeling that it will, eventually." What in the world did she mean by that? I got a cold chill up my spine.

We continued rummaging through the house. About 8:00 p.m. I noticed Cassie was looking a little pale and had probably over-exerted herself.

"Let's order some pizza and just stay here for the night. Cassie, you need some rest. Tomorrow we'll get a fresh start and figure out the next step." She agreed and lay down on the sofa until the pizza arrived.

The doorbell rang, I opened the door to a young, maybe 17 year old guy holding our dinner. I gave him the money with a tip and took hold of the pizza box. He was very polite but seemed to have trouble taking his hand away from the box.

"Um, thank you and uh, have a nice night." He stammered a little and started to walk backward toward the two steps of the porch. I realized at that moment that he was going fall off the porch!

"Hey, be careful! You're gonna…" Too late. He had turned to step down but missed the first step and found himself face first on the cement!

"Are you okay?!" I quickly put the pizza box on the ground and ran down to see if the kid was hurt.

"Yeah, I'm good. Embarrassed but ok. You two enjoy your pizza and I'm going to go crawl into a hole." He had a very sad grin on his face as he ran to his car.

"I think it's my fault. I came to the door behind you. I think it threw him that he was looking at twins, poor kid." Cassie picked up the pizza and we went inside laughing.

After dinner we decided to turn in and get a fresh start in the morning.

"Go on to bed. I'll sleep out here on the sofa. Cassie nodded and walked to Damien's room. I had never seen her so sad and lost. I was fairly sure it wasn't all about Damien. She probably couldn't stop thinking of the horrible ordeal those criminals had put her through.

I tried to sleep but finally gave up and spent the rest of the night reading Damien's journals, hoping some answers would jump at me. The journals were very interesting – at least the parts I could actually understand. His descriptions of the island; the tribal people; the forests; huts, etc. were so vivid that I felt like I was there with him. I grabbed the last journal and my hope was fading. I found myself reading it slowly, like that would make the journal magically grow more pages. A third of the way through, my hope began to return...

> *May 6th*
>
> *I'm losing track of time. Hours turn to days, days to months. I don't care that my life back home is going on without me. I could spend a lifetime out here and never lose interest or have enough studies.*
>
> *Today was a typical day, and the language barrier has become smaller. I can almost speak their language now, at least enough to get through a conversation.*
>
> *I've also noticed that my powers, or whatever they are, have gotten stronger, more intense. I am completely*

mystified as to how I obtained them or what they are. So far, I can read people's minds and my sense of my surroundings is very intense. I can hear and see so much more clearly. I have learned how to turn off thoughts of others, as I still feel that's invading their privacy and makes me feel like a peeping Tom. It's so strange but the only thing I can come up with is there's something in the food or drinks. They have this herbal drink that I've consumed large quantities of – maybe that's the answer.

Tonight the Chief invited me to his hut for dinner with his family, which he has done only twice since I've been here. Dinner was good, and the conversation was better. They introduced a new drink to me that I can't quite describe. The Chief told me that their ancestors would drink this before battles or when something was about to happen. I asked him why he gave me the drink. His answer didn't sit very well with me, but I decided to shrug it off and enjoy the evening. All he would say is that I earned it. What does that mean? Maybe in a few days I can get him to elaborate. Before I leave, I need to get some samples of all these drinks and take them back with me.

May 9th

There is tension in the tribe. I am writing this during daylight hours, as I don't want to forget anything. I walked up the path a bit so they wouldn't see me. I'm not sure what is going on, but I am starting to get a little nervous. When the tribe speaks I try to hear or understand what they are saying, but they almost seem scared. I've been trying to read the Chief's mind, but it's like a brick wall and I can't get in. I tried others' minds, but the same thing keeps happening.

I also have an eerie feeling that I'm being watched. Last night I stepped out of my tent as I couldn't sleep, and nearly had a heart attack. In the bushes were two red glowing – well, they looked like eyes! I'm wondering if that drink they gave me has some long-lasting side effects and I'm starting to hallucinate. I walked closer to the bush and heard rustling noises, then the eyes – or whatever they were – disappeared! I think I'm losing my mind, and maybe it's time to get home. Someone's coming…

May 9ᵗʰ later (they're all in bed)

Okay, now I know I have to get out of here. I can't explain it, I'm not scared – well, not yet but I know I have to go. But how do I leave? I don't know how to reach the captain of the ship. He probably showed on the expected day and left when I didn't show. I'm sure no one is looking for me by now. Even if they had put a search party on the island, there is no way they would have found me. What do I do?

Oh my God, there are those eyes again! This time I can see they are eyes! I don't know what they belong to, I can't see the body. I'm signing off for now so I can get everything packed up while the tribe is sleeping and find my way to shore. I'm hoping my boat is still on the beach and at least I can get part way and try to flag down a ship.

May 10ᵗʰ

I don't know how I did it, but I finally found my way to the boat. It took a long time and the sun was just starting to rise, but I made it. I'm drifting at sea and praying a ship comes along. I'm thankful that the weather is clear and the water is calm. I can see for miles, and the sky is a beautiful turquoise. The only problem is, it's hot!

I think I see a boat! Can it be possible? It is! I have to try to get their attention! It's a yacht, I think.

At that moment, I remembered something Jesse had told me! Damien worked for a university or was transferring to one, I can't remember but I had to figure it out! I grabbed my laptop and Googled 'Universities'. There were too many and looking at a few names didn't ring any bells. In fact, I wasn't sure he had ever mentioned which one. I looked at the clock to see if it would be too early to wake up Cassie. I had to find out what university Damien spoke of. Okay, maybe too early to wake her up, it was 4:30 a.m.! I had not gotten any sleep!

"Fine, I'll lie down for awhile then ask her when she gets up."

The next thing I knew, Cassie was waking me up.

"What time is it?"

"It's 11:30. I would've woken you earlier but you seemed so peaceful."

"Eleven thirty! Cassie, what is the name of the university that Damien worked for? I think I found a huge clue in his journal!" I sat up as Cassie sat next to me.

"Well, he was going to transfer to Boston and start with NE University or something like that. I'm not sure if he was actually working for them yet."

I flipped open my laptop and Googled the university. I found the number for the Department of Biology and dialed the number. A lady answered the phone and I explained the connection Cassie and I had to Damien. I told her he had made it off that island but went missing again.

The lady knew him and had wondered what had happened to him. She explained that the university did everything they could to find him but had to let it go and let the authorities take over. She never heard another word about Damien until I called. She really wanted to help and gave me the name and number of the captain of the research vessel Damien was aboard. I called the number and got his voicemail. I left a detailed message and left my number.

Cassie and I decided to go into town and get some breakfast while we waited for the captain to return my call. She knew of a little diner not too far away. I wasn't very hungry but knew we both needed all the energy we could get.

We returned to the house and I gathered Damien's journals and put them in my duffel bag. The sighting of the yacht was the last entry. Cassie sat on the couch in the living room and turned on the television.

The news was on all local stations, with the same reports of the last brutal killings. The deaths were definitely creepy, especially since there didn't seem to be any way of running or escaping the mysterious killer. It started in Nevada – why?

I needed to keep my mind busy while waiting for the captain to call back so I grabbed a book off the shelf in Damien's office which was his second bedroom. As I turned toward the door, I glanced at his mahogany desk. How did I not think of this earlier?! What a dork! His important papers, calendars, schedules, research, and anything else he was working on would be in this room. Duh!

TJ already ransacked this room but hopefully Damien had a hiding place for items that TJ missed. All the drawers to the desk had been broken into so I didn't bother with them. I started feeling around the sides of the desk to see if there was a secret compartment or something. I moved the desk, which about gave me a hernia because of the weight, and at the bottom near the floor it looked like a crack in the desk. I felt around the crack and pushed my fingers around the whole parameter. Feeling under the desk between the archway of the leg, was a button. I pushed it and out popped a skinny secret drawer! I pulled out some sort of paper, it was a map that was folded neatly. Ha! TJ missed it! I grabbed it and ran into the living room. Cassie was still mesmerized by the news stories. I sat next to her and spread out the map on the coffee table.

"What is that?"

"There is a secret drawer in his desk that TJ missed! It's some sort of map, probably the island. Help me figure this out." Cassie nodded and turned the television off.

Damien had marked the map with a red pen and traced an area around South America. There was a small "x" a little north of Venezuela but it didn't make any sense. There was no land where the "x" was, only water. I didn't care, that had to be the location of the island he had been on. I was sure we would find the guys on that island! I had no idea what made me think they had been taken there, but I knew in my gut that the island held the answers.

After explaining my theory to Cassie, I paused so she could tell me I was crazy but she didn't.

"Yeah, maybe you're right Mandy." Cassie was still very quiet, seemingly calm but I knew she was far from that.

We leaned back on the couch and waited for the Captain's phone call. My mind drifted to the dreadful day on the beach. It seemed like it was months ago, but it was only a couple of days ago. I let my mind wander to some quiet moments that Jesse and I had shared, and how quickly I had fallen for this stranger. We had been through so much in such a short time, and when he disappeared he took a large part of me with him. Just as I started remembering the horseback ride on the beach, the phone rang.

"Hello?"

"Miss Tagama?"

"Yes this is Mandy, is this Andrew?" My heart was racing.

"Yes, it is. What can I do for you?" His voice was deep and raspy.

"I hope you can help me. About a year ago you dropped off a man named Damien Balcombe on an island. He and his twin brother have disappeared, and I think they were taken back to that island. Please sir, I am begging you to take me and my sister to that island!" I paused to give the poor man a chance to respond. There were several long seconds of silence before he spoke.

"I remember Damien, but I can't help you. I am sorry. I almost lost my job over that delivery, and I can't take any chances. I really am sorry but I can't..." He hung up. I sat there in shock for a minute.

Fine, if he won't help we'll charter a boat. We are going to the island. I grabbed the map and settled in the dining room so I wouldn't disturb Cassie and her fascination with the news. I spread the map on the table and went to work. After numerous phone calls, and being referred to number after number, I began to think it was hopeless and we wouldn't find a boat.

Finally, I got a man on the phone, Mike, who told me he would be happy to take us to the location. He's in Miami, Florida and told me if we could make it there, he would take us and try to find this island. I thanked him and took his contact information. I told him I would call him later today after making plane reservations.

I made all the arrangements then found Cassie watching the news, of course. I muted the TV so I could explain the plans.

I walked into the room and Cassie looked like she was in a trance. She quickly snapped out of it when I started my explanation.

"Sheesh, when did you do all this?!"

"The last couple of hours, goof ball. You've been glued to this TV. A tornado could've come through here and you still wouldn't have taken your eyes off the TV." We laughed and I un-muted the Television.

"You can change the channel, I've seen enough of this horror. It's like watching a plane crash over and over. It's horrible but you can't turn away. I've always wondered why that is."

I put my finger on the "up/down" button on the remote and almost changed the channel, when I spotted something in the bushes behind the reporter.

"What's wrong Mandy?"

"I saw something in that bush." Damien had a DVR so I could rewind live television.

"Watch, in the bush behind that reporter."

"What did you see?"

"I don't know except I've seen it before. They look like red glowing eyes. When you were in the hospital Jesse and I saw something like that by the parking lot. Jesse didn't know what they were either." I'm sure Cassie thought I was going crazy, but she stayed next to me as we tried to see the "eyes" again. And there they were!

"There! Did you see them?" It was as if they kept blinking!

"I think I saw something but not sure if they're eyes. Maybe it's a glare from the cameras or the sun or something." I changed the channel to see if there was a different angle from a different reporter, but no luck. I kept trying more channels.

"Wait a second!" I remembered something Damien had written in one of his journals so I ran to my bag to retrieve it.

I sat down next to Cassie and found the entry where he had seen the same thing!

"What does it mean?" Cassie had fear in her eyes as she asked me the question.

"I don't know but something tells me that it's connected. I wasn't sure what to think when you said that yesterday about these murders but maybe you are right, maybe it's all connected." I closed the journal and sat further back on the couch.

The rest of the day was spent watching more TV, reading and mind wandering. We ate the rest of the pizza for dinner then turned in early so we would be rested for the upcoming trip. I decided to take the guest room and sleep on a real bed, since I didn't get much sleep the previous night.

The room was small, but decorated with rich colors and contemporary furniture. The house was quiet, which made it more difficult to turn off my brain. I lay on my side staring into the darkness and let my thoughts stray on Jesse and the good times we had the last few weeks, which helped me fall into a deep sleep. I dreamed of the intimate moments we had, the laughter and the horseback ride we shared. Then, my dreams turned dark and I felt like I was falling into a twisting funnel. Wind was swirling around me as I was being thrown like a rag doll against the sides of the funnel, but it stopped abruptly and my mind was pitch black and quiet until...

I was at my ranch in the middle of the dressage arena. I looked...sad. I gave instructions to my students as they circled their horses around me. My students looked worried, but I wasn't sure why. They stared at me from their mounts. I seemed to be going through the motions of a lesson, but wasn't really into it. Why? I loved teaching and loved my students. Then, their were diverted to the outside of the arena. I no longer stood in the arena, but outside of it. The students stopped their horses at the fence and stared at me. I was standing in the grass and looking up toward the house. What was I doing? It didn't take long for the answer, yet it still did not make sense.

"Mandy, can you hear me? Mandy, it's Jesse."

"What the...?! Jesse?!" I wheeled around, looking at the arena, then the barn, toward the house...nothing. I spun around again in all directions, then knelt down on the grass, sobbing.

"I can't go through this again! The voices had stopped! What do you want with me?! Leave me alone! I did everything you asked! You're not Jesse! I don't know who you are but go away!" My mind went blank.

I woke with a start, shaking and sweating. I sat up in the bed and realized I had been crying. My face and pillow were soaked. I got out of bed and went into the bathroom to clean myself up. I couldn't stop shaking.

What the hell was that? Voices, plural? What voices? I know it was just a dream but I did not recognize that voice. It was an eerie, creepy voice. Okay, the ones I'm hearing right now that's me and I'm going out of my mind. I've got to find Jesse. Mandy, get yourself together and go back to bed.

I walked out of the bathroom and just as I started to climb back into bed...

"You're absolutely right, it's NOT Jesse talking to you."

What?! I spun around facing the doorway. The shaking came back in full force.

"Who's there?!" I stood still next to the bed, staring at the doorway.

"Mandy, get a hold of yourself!" When I realized I was speaking out loud I crawled under the covers.

Chapter 2

The next morning Cassie and I gathered our things and headed to the airport. We checked our bags, got through security and found our gate. I was actually getting tired of airports, hotels, and especially rental cars, but we had no choice. We had to try; try to find the guys and bring them home safe and sound.

Neither of us said much on the plane, and I had given Cassie the window seat. She stared out the window the entire trip. She fell asleep a couple of times, but not very deeply as she woke up every time the flight attendant walked by or something was said over the intercom.

We landed in Miami. Mike had told me he would meet us outside baggage claim and had given me a description of himself and his car.

Cassie and I stood outside baggage claim and looked for Mike's gray Toyota Tundra.

"What does his car look like, Mandy?"

"He said it's a little gray truck." I looked at every single vehicle, bus, shuttle, everything. Nothing. No Mike.

"Maybe he's stuck in traffic." Cassie said as she sat on a nearby bench.

"Maybe." I had a sick feeling inside my stomach that grew stronger as the seconds became minutes.

I tried his cell phone and the alternate number he had given me. The call to his cell went straight through to voicemail, and the other number just kept ringing. He had also given me the number of his charter business. I left him a voicemail and decided we would wait a little longer before panicking.

After an hour I had had enough.

"Okay, let's take a cab to the marina. He gave me the business address and maybe someone there would know where he is." We jumped into the first cab we saw and gave the driver the address.

When we arrived at the marina, I asked the driver to wait while we tried to find Mike. The door to the business was locked, and we didn't see anyone around.

"Now what?" Cassie's voice had a sense of urgency and I knew she was getting worried and scared.

"It's okay, we'll find him and if not him, someone else who will take us to the island. I'm not giving up." Just then a man came around from the other side of the building.

"Excuse me, are you Mike?"

"No. Are you looking for Mike Powell?"

"I'm not sure of his last name. We chartered a boat from him."

"That's Mike Powell. I haven't seen him today, but he told me yesterday he had a charter gig today that would have him gone for a week or so. I'm watching over things while he's away. I'm John, by the way." He reached out and we shook hands.

"I'm Mandy and this is my sister, Cassie. We're actually the 'gig' he told you about. He was supposed to pick us up at the airport but never showed, so we took a cab out here."

"Wow, that's not like Mike. He's never late and doesn't forget things. Come on in and I'll make some calls. Don't worry, we'll find him and then you two lovely ladies can be on your way." He unlocked the door to the shop and we all went inside. I remembered we left the cab driver sitting outside but before I could grab the doorknob John intervened.

"Do you have bags in the cab? I'll send the guy on his way and get your bags if you want."

"That would be great, thank you." I handed John some money for the cab driver and Cassie took a seat in the lobby.

He came back inside, put our bags at our feet, and handed me our change. I smiled and thanked him.

"I'll make some coffee, then go make those calls. Mike has to be around somewhere." He smiled back at us and disappeared after making some coffee. The smell of coffee soothed us as the little machine made its soft, gurgling sounds. Cassie and I sat in silence while we waited for John to return. He was nice-looking – mid-thirties; tall; thin except for a slight belly, but not fat. He had wavy, brown hair and brown eyes. He seemed genuinely nice but also a little concerned for his friend, who obviously never missed a "gig".

John returned to the lobby after a few short minutes and looked a little pale, even through his tanned skin.

"Um, I have some – well, uh…Mike is dead." My blood turned cold, but my skin felt hot. We all stared at each other and then John spoke again, trying to choke back tears.

"I called his neighbor, and he could barely get the words out to tell me what happened. Steve, the neighbor, said Mike took the boat out last night to see if it needed any work before your trip. Steve is Mike's emergency contact, and the police showed up at his house in the middle of the night to inform him that they found the wreckage a mile offshore. A witness called the police and said they heard an explosion and saw flames out in the water. It turned out to be Mike's boat." John turned his head to the side, trying to hide his tears.

"I can't believe I didn't even notice his boat was gone this morning. What kind of friend am I?" I walked over and hugged him. I couldn't shake the feeling that the killings on the news, my nightmare last night, and the guys' disappearance had something to do with Mike's death.

John apologized and said he needed a minute. He pulled back from me and told us to stay in the lobby. He walked to the back and was gone for 15-20 minutes. When he returned, he said "I'm going to clear my schedule and take you on my boat. I called Tammy and booked you a room for tonight. She owns the local motel up the road and feels horrible about everything. She said the room is on her and we'll leave first thing in the morning." John grabbed our bags and headed outside. Under normal circumstances I would have told this kind man not to worry about it and to take care of himself and Mike's family, if he had any; but Jesse and Damien needed us to find them and we needed John. I felt selfish, but couldn't worry about that now.

We thanked him profusely and followed him outside. He locked the door then told us to wait as he pulled his truck around.

"John."

"Yeah." He stopped but didn't turn around.

"I'm so sorry about Mike and if we weren't so worried about our friends I would tell you to forget about it and go our separate ways. I just don't know what else to do and Mike was the only one available. But I am truly sorry."

"It's no problem and thank you." He proceeded forward toward the side parking lot.

Cassie was sobbing, and I took her by the shoulders and sat her back in the chair that sat outside the window of the shop. I tried to reassure her that everything would be okay, but it was hard since I wasn't sure myself. I sat in the chair beside Cassie and kept my arm around her shoulder.

We sat there for a few minutes, when all of a sudden my head began to pound and throb. It felt as if all the blood vessels would burst through my skull – then it stopped as quickly as it started…

"Mandy, I just had a vision of you and Cassie! GO HOME PLEASE! Things are too dangerous and I'm not sure what's going on out there, but you're in danger. I don't have much time, but Damien and I are…"

"How do you keep busting through?! You're not supposed to have access to certain powers right now! Anyway, Mandy listen to him. If you take this next boat it will have the same consequences as Mike's! Your new friend, your sister and yourself will go down with it! Go home, both of you. Otherwise, a lot more people will die needlessly. You will not go to the island! Forget about Jesse if you know what's good for you and Cassie. GO HOME NOW!"

Both the voices stopped. Voices?! What the…? The first one was Jesse but the second voice was – that scary one from my nightmare. As I lifted my head out of my hands, I realized I scared Cassie as I pulled my head out of hands.

"Mandy, what's going on? Are you okay? Mandy!" I stood up and hugged her.

"I'm fine, I just got this really bad headache, but it's gone now." I didn't know what to do. Did I really just hear Jesse's voice again, and some creepy insane second voice threatening us? Do we just go home or do I decide it's a sign of insanity and continue on with our rescue plan? Right at this second, the only thing that made sense was to call Mom and Dad and put Cassie on a plane to stay with them for a while. I would feel better if my sister was safe, then I could really concentrate on my next move. If that was Jesse, then I know he must be okay for the time being. *If that was Jesse…did I fall into the Twilight Zone again? This is getting way too weird and dangerous. I have to get Cassie out of here.*

I said, "Cassie, you need to go to Mom and Dad's. I'm going to call them and see if they'll drive down and get you."

"What?! NO! I'm staying with you. We need to find Damien and Jesse!"

"You're still recovering. This is way too much. I should've thought of this when we left Nevada. We will be in the middle of the ocean for days, and if you relapse there is absolutely no medical care at all! This is not up for discussion! You are going to Mom and Dad's. I will keep you updated. I will find them and our first stop after that will be Florida to pick you up." She gave me the 'whatever' look that teens give their parents and leaned back in the chair.

I found John and told him we may have to wait one extra day. I didn't know if my parents could leave today but hoped they could.

"Tell you what. Throw your stuff in my truck and I'll take you to the motel and you can wait on your parents in comfort. I'll get some stuff taken care of around here. I'll check in with you sometime tomorrow and see what the plan is. I'm sure Mindy would love to have you an extra night."

I called mom and dad when we got to the motel. Just as I knew they would be, they were thrilled to have at least one of their daughters with them. They tried to talk me into joining Cassie, at least for a few days. I told them a lie, which made me feel guilty, and said I needed to get back to the ranch. Cassie and I had discussed what to tell them and decided it was in their best interest to be left in the dark on the sordid details.

"Well, they will be here in the morning so we might as well relax and enjoy the Florida sunshine."

Cassie and I spent the day walking around window shopping in the cute shops and markets. When we were tired we picked up some food at a little café down the street from the motel and took it back to eat. We watched television the rest of the evening.

"Well Cassie, I'm gonna turn in. Good night."

"Good night." I could tell she was still irritated that she wasn't going but knew I was right.

I climbed into my queen sized bed and lay there for a while. It was impossible to turn off my brain, but eventually fell into a deep slumber...

My dream began calm and peaceful. I was riding Zamira on the hillside. He was feeling good and appreciated the freedom from the arena. We cantered along the trail up a tree-lined hill. It was a clear day with a light summer breeze blowing through my hair. I felt free, which is the feeling I get every time I ride.

But the dream took a dark turn...again. I wasn't riding any longer, I was on a boat; not a big boat but larger than a speedboat. John, was driving. I stepped down to the main level and put my hands on the railing, watching the water swirl and fold after us. So far, things seemed normal and quiet but the serenity didn't last long...I suddenly felt shaking beneath my feet. I looked up toward the cabin to find John. His back was to me and he seemed fine. I then looked to the east and at first saw nothing but blue sky and calm seas. I stared out over the swirling ocean and saw them! Those red glowing lights – eyes, or whatever – but they were in the air! They blinked on and off!

"I told you more people would die if you continued this investigation." Suddenly I was grabbed and pulled into the air! I flew straight up and looked below me. The boat got smaller, and I wasn't sure what this 'voice' meant. Did he mean that I was going to die? Just then the boat exploded beneath me! Yellow flames and black smoke shot up toward us! Pieces of the boat shot out in all directions. The gust from the explosion burst upward and a piece of wooden shrapnel flew past me so close that it grazed my hair!

Then the dream shifted to another scene. It was Jesse and Damien, lying in grass. It was as if I were hovering over their bodies. I was floating over a field and they were lying there...sleeping.

"Jesse! Wake up! Wake up, you're in danger! Jesse!" They didn't move, and I began to float away from them. I struggled and tried to put my feet on the ground, but I just kept going higher and higher, and then both of them suddenly imploded! I screamed and thrashed, trying to

reach them, but couldn't get away from whatever force was holding me in the air.
"NO!"

My eyes flew open, and once again I was sweating and trembling. I sat straight up then looked over at Cassie. She was still sleeping, thank goodness. What did this mean?! Did that voice mean he would not only kill John, but Jesse and Damien too? Were Jesse and Damien already dead? NO, that can't be true!

I looked at the clock on the bedside table – it was 6:00 a.m. What do I do? Give up on finding them so no else dies? So they wouldn't die? Keep trying and risk dooming everyone I hire to a fiery death? Then I thought, maybe it's just my crazy imagination due to Mike's dying in an explosion. Yes, that had to be it. I've been on an insane roller coaster for weeks, and the stress has finally caught up to me.

I decided to take a hot shower. The shower was exhilarating. I stood in the hot water and pretended it was a waterfall and Jesse was there with me. I closed my eyes and pictured it, but each time I thought of Jesse in a warm and loving moment, my thoughts were interrupted and the pounding in my head started again!

I'M NOT KIDDING OR PLAYING GAMES! Stop this
search or John will die! I will kill each poor soul you hire.
Don't test me on this. Go home and continue with your
life. Forget Jesse and Damien – you will never see them
again. I will kill them if you don't STOP!"

"FINE! If you want me to believe that you're real, then you need to
show proof that Jesse and Damien are safe." Oh my God, I'm talking to
a voice in my head. Part of me really thought I was losing it, but the other part remembered some of the abilities that Jesse and Damien had acquired. How they received those abilities was still a mystery. I had no choice but to believe that whoever or whatever was holding the guys could harm them or me and my sister. I decided

it wasn't as impossible as I had believed, when I remembered how Jesse made us invisible to escape Cassie's kidnappers. I wasn't sure what else he could do, but why not someone else having the ability to speak to me through my mind?

The more I considered all this, the more I realized that it probably was Jesse 'talking' to me the day they disappeared and yesterday. But who is this other strange voice? Could he be holding the guys captive? Then another thought barreled into my head…if this 'voice' spoke to me and knew of decisions I was making, then what if he were able to see me as well? Crap! I'm standing in the shower with no clothes on!

Even though the idea sounded ridiculous and creepy, I wasn't taking the chance – ugh – which meant what… I could never take a shower again? I hurried and dried myself off, then quickly put on jeans and a t-shirt. I sat on the bed and realized the 'voice' hadn't answered me. Maybe I am losing my mind, but apparently the 'voice' sensed my wavering and decided to remind me. My head began to throb again with excruciating pain. I thought my head would implode and then remembered that Jesse would go through this occasionally. Did this 'voice' speak to him too? I held my head and prayed the pain would stop. When it did, I saw them…

> *"Damien, what was that?"*
> *"What was what?"*
> *"That noise."* Jesse and Damien stood in a field of tall grass.
> *"Mandy?!, Mandy, is that you?! I can feel you, Baby. Wait, why can I feel your presence all of a sudden? Are you girls okay? Nikias, I swear if you hurt either of them I will kill you!!"*
> *"Hey, your girl wanted proof of your safety so I am showing her you're both okay. But you better convince her to stop the insane search. I thought you could talk some sense into her so I wouldn't have to kill her, or others she*

loves. I suggest you convince your precious Mandy to go home and pretend she never met you.

Hey – I just thought of something else that may be more fun and...hmmm, maybe safer for your beloved. I could take her memory of the last few weeks away! She wouldn't remember meeting you or Damien, the kidnapping, the adventures of finding her sister! This would be SO much more fun! She would wake up in a few minutes in a strange hotel, and wouldn't remember how or when she arrived. Mandy, you would be very confused for a while, but eventually you will continue with your life.

That would be awesome! That would mess with both of you at the same time! Aw, but I would also have to take Cassie's memories of the first few weeks as well, and come to think of it, her parents'. Sheesh, this is getting complicated, but it would be so worth it!"

"Nikias! I will convince her to go home! Don't do anything else! Mandy, please, you have to listen to him and GO HOME! He means what he says and he will take your memories from you! I'm okay and so is Damien. I will make my way back to you someday, I promise!" *He was spinning in circles in the grass trying to locate me. I screamed out at him but for some reason he couldn't hear me. Then I screamed at the other voice, 'leave me and my sister alone! I will do what you say and go home!" No one responded...*

It stopped suddenly.

"No! Please, let me see more! I promise I will stop looking and go home, but let me talk to him! PLEASE!" *Who is Nikias?*

"Okay, you win, Nikias! Whoever or whatever you are, I'm going home! But Jesse and Damien had better be alive and well! Please leave me and my sister alone! I'm going home."

Wise decision. I haven't decided about the whole memory thing yet. I think I'll let all of you stew about that one for a while. This is going to be so much fun!

"You're evil!" I was going to have to listen to him. I didn't know how I would go on, but I had to believe I would see Jesse again. I was going to keep my end of the bargain, but that didn't mean the mysterious voice would keep his...

Chapter 3

Montana

Three Months Later

"Mandy, I swear you'd be late to your own funeral! Your next class starts in twenty minutes!" Becca yelled from the edge of the Dressage arena. I could hear the aggravation in her voice. Becca is my right hand lady and I'd be lost without her. She keeps me in line – a full-time job. She is so much more than my secretary; only 4 years older than me at 29, she is my friend, colleague and savior.

"Okay, I'm on my way after this one jump, I promise." Becca rolled her eyes and headed back to the office located in the barn. I turned my 16.2 hand sorrel Hanoverian stallion toward the one jump we had had problems with a few minutes ago.

When I bought Zamira I had high hopes for the two of us, but daily life had taken over. I have no regrets about that. I have devoted my life to this ranch and the students and he has become a vital part of that.

I looked between his twitching ears and studied the upcoming jump. How many strides would he have to take? Would he position himself correctly and take the jump on time, or would he leap too soon? Those questions and more went through my head on every approach to a jump.

"Okay, Zamira, one more time and then you can retire for today." I tightened the reins in my fingers and Zamira began to side-step slightly with anticipation as he sensed the moment. I barely squeezed my calves and he moved smoothly into a canter. Then I moved my upper body forward. Closer to his head, and readied my hands in position.

"You can do this, big boy."

The jump was just five strides ahead, and I could feel the confidence in him as his ears twitched back and forth, his body like steel. I hugged my body closer into his neck. We felt like one as I moved my hands down a little more on the reins. The front half of his body slowly rose to the height of the four-foot jump, and we glided smoothly over the top. I peeked down for a split second and witnessed the jump and ground integrating into one scene. Zamira's front hooves hit the ground with a subtle thud, while his back half and hooves slid gracefully behind us. Success! I rubbed his neck firmly and hugged as much of it as I could get my arms around.

"Good job, boy! How about those treats I promised you?" I let him prance and side-step around the arena one last time. Cars start pulling into the long drive that led to the barn.

There's my cue, boy. My class will be starting and Becca will have my head on a platter if I'm late." I jumped off – no small task – and handed him over to Tony, my barn manager.

"Would you cool him off? But leave the treats for me, okay?" I handed the reins to Tony and he nodded in agreement.

I jogged up the grassy slope to the barn to greet my advanced students. They stood in two partial circles in front of the barn. The girls; Kristin, Laura, Jessica, Amy and Jennifer whispering about the boys they liked and giggling. The three boys, Zach, Jacob and Gerrhett, stood goofing off on the other side of the barn. The boys were clowns but excellent riders. All of these students were16 and 17 years old and I'd had all eight of them since I started this business three years ago. I had grown to care for each and every one of them.

I noticed all the students were here except one. Four months ago I had gained a ninth student – Samantha, Sam for short. She was 17 years old and kept to herself, very quiet but an excellent rider. Sam sometimes had a dark look about her, but her light amber eyes revealed the frightened child who had been inside her for a long time. She tried to put on a brave, tough front without saying the words. She was one of the most natural kids on a horse I'd ever seen.

Sam lives with foster parents and their case worker recommended riding lessons with me to help her focus on positive behavior. Before Sam was put into the system, she had been involved in horses and English riding. The foster parents worried that Sam would get hurt and were reluctant at first, but now they are thrilled with the improvement in her attitude.

I wanted to put her in my Intermediate class to start and see where her strengthand weaknesses were but she convinced me to let her ride in my advanced class the first day. When I saw her ride the first day, wow! There is nothing intermediate about her. She would have been bored to death in my Intermediate class. Sam didn't really fit in with the other students though, who came from well-to-do families – very privileged but good kids. Sam was quiet and kept to herself and the others eventually accepted her.

"Okay, goobers – get your horses saddled and meet me in the arena in fifteen minutes. Anyone who is late will unsaddle and ride the rest of the lesson bareback." I winked at the girls and headed to the barn, but stopped short when I saw Sam pulling in with her foster parents.

"Hey Sam, you ride Molly today. Get her saddled and in the arena in fifteen." Sam was the only student who didn't have her own horse, so I let her ride one of mine each week.

She didn't look right though. "Sam, are you okay?"

"Uh-huh." She kept her head down as she answered and kept walking toward the barn. I decided she would talk about it when she was ready. I walked briskly to the office to check in with Becca then headed down to the arena.

Today's lesson would consist of Dressage, no jumping. I couldn't wait to see the looks on their faces when I informed them of that. Teenagers tend to get bored easily and want to only have fun. I guess conditioning was not as fun as jumping. We have a teaching show scheduled here in two weeks and I wanted the kids and horses ready, both physically and mentally. I moved some jumps out of the way and brought out the 2x4 boards Tony had brought for us earlier. I placed them two feet apart parallel to each other for the horses to step over.

"My lesson plan? Where did I put it?" I started running back toward the office when Becca showed up at the gate with the plan in hand.

"Becca, what would I do without you?"

"You're kidding right?! You'd be lost. You'd be late for every class, the students would give up on you and the business would perish." She took a deep breath. "Can I have a raise?" she said, laughing and rolling her eyes.

"You're a funny, funny girl...don't push it." Just then the kids showed up with two minutes to spare. Dang it, I had hoped for at least one to have the tough task of riding bareback today!

"Okay today is something that you LOVE to do – Dressage, no jumping...Yay!" The girls rolled their eyes and the guys groaned, like typical teenagers. However, the class went smoothly and they all got a good workout.

"All right, cool them down and I'll see you next week. In the meantime, get out here as much as you can and get some practice for our show in two weeks."

They all lined up single file to head out the gate and I followed behind Sam. "Hey Sam, would you hang back a minute?" Sam whirled the little Quarter Horse around to face me.

"I want you to ride Tobias in the show. Can you come back this Friday so we can get both of you ready?"

"Really?! Tobias?! YEAH!! I would love to ride him!" I had never seen her that animated about anything - but it didn't last long. Her whole body language changed. She slumped over in her saddle and said "Um, if I'm still here." She hung her head and started to turn around.

"Wait ...what? Sam, what do you mean, 'if you're still here'? What's going on?"

"My foster parents have had me for almost a year and as you know, that's way longer than they're supposed to have a kid. My case worker is trying to extend it, but they might have to move me somewhere else. They act pretty upset but I don't know, they'll probably be relieved to get rid of me." I could tell she was trying hard not to cry...she didn't like to show emotion.

I didn't know what to say – I felt like someone had punched me in the stomach. I had become very attached to Sam.

"I'll talk to your foster parents and see what's going on. Get Molly cooled down and I'll see ya Friday morning." Sam wheeled Molly around and cantered up the hill to the barn.

I watched her as she cantered to the barn. A hundred different thoughts went tumbling through my mind. I needed to talk to the case worker, but would talk to the foster parents first. Since I had been a social worker after college for a brief moment, maybe I could get custody of Sam. *Whoa, did I just consider custody of a teenager?!*

I walked up the hill past the barn doorway and saw the girls hosing down their horses, giggling. I went to the office, which was around the corner from the doorway.

Becca met me at the office door. "Mandy, the show is in two weeks! I still don't have all the judges hired and I'm having trouble getting the ribbons printed. The company's giving some song and dance about how busy they are! I have the ambulance lined up, but they're not sure if they can be there for the first 30 minutes. The food vendor hasn't gotten back to me yet and I've left umpteen messages! And that's just for THIS show – I haven't even started the calls for the next two shows!" She started thumbing through paperwork on her desk. "And if you line up shows back to back again I'm going to run over you with my car!" She laughed and handed me a stack of messages that had come in while I was out with the girls.

"Becca, breathe! It's okay we'll get it all done. Haven't our shows always come together? I only have my ten a.m. beginner class tomorrow, so I can work on some of this stuff.

Oh, I'm having Sam ride Tobias in the show so she's coming Friday morning for some extra riding. I think he needs it more than she does."

"That's fine, you have an open schedule Friday anyway." Becca said while still giving me an evil eye.

"We're done for the day, so why don't you go on home and enjoy your day off tomorrow. And again, breathe." She gave me her 'I can't believe you just said that' look but grinned and gathered her stuff to leave.

"Ok, I'll see you Thursday. Breathing, I'm breathing." She winked at me then walked out the door.

I sat at Becca's big oak desk that was pushed against the wall next to the door. I stared at the mess, trying to decide where to start. I couldn't get Sam out of my head so put that first on my agenda.

I needed the phone number for Sam's foster parents and began thumbing through Becca's rolodex. I also found the paperwork for the show that was shoved into a manila folder to the right of the computer monitor. I put that onto my own desk so I would remember to make those calls tomorrow after my class.

My desk sat on the other side of the room, and as I placed the folder on top of it, I realized what a slob I had become. There were papers, sticky notes, folders and paperclips all over the place and some on the floor. I reached to my right and opened the big file drawer to retrieve the blank lesson plan sheets that Becca had made for me on a spreadsheet. I sat there staring at the spreadsheet, then remembered that I had needed the number for Sam's foster parents and hadn't followed through with that. *Price I pay when I keep my mind too busy…I start too many things at once. I need to talk to the case worker first anyway and she would be gone for the day.*

"Well, this isn't going to work. I'm not getting anything done." I decided to give Zamira the treats I had promised him and get some chores done before tackling the paperwork. Physical work would take my mind off Sam. I grabbed a bag of my favorite candy, Skittles, from my desk drawer and started walking to the door. I stopped for a brief second and looked at the bag of candy. For several months every time I picked up a bag, something gnawed at me and I haven't been able to figure it out.

The past three months had been a little strange. I felt as if part of my mind was in a mist or a fog. There are a few weeks that I can't get a grip on. I remember them as normal days but I feel like those weeks were a dream.

I didn't understand why I felt this way. My life was as normal as ever. I wake up; teach; joke around with my students and employees; ride one of the horses; then run up the hill to the house and shower. I eat dinner; watch TV or read; then off to bed - just to get up in the morning and do it all over again. Once in a while I feel decadent and venture into town to get supplies, grab something to eat and a movie. Nothing out of the ordinary but still something not right and I will dwell on the strangeness for a while, then forget and go on with my life. But other times it would take a little longer to get over. I would feel this overwhelming sense of loss. Why? What loss?

I headed into the barn. Zamira heard me come in and immediately started pawing the ground in his stall. He was a big teddy bear and my first horse here at Zamira's Dream. I saw Tony walking toward me down the breezeway.

"Hi, Mandy. I have Romulus' stall to clean, then heading home. Everyone's in, fed and watered." Zamira continued to paw the ground, demanding my attention.

"Thanks, Tony. Go on home and I'll take care of Romulus."

"Are you sure?"

"Absolutely. Get home early for a change and give Becca a shock." Tony laughed and headed out the barn door. Tony and Becca started dating shortly after the business opened and now lived together. They were the perfect couple and I hoped someday I would find that kind of love.

I continued to Zamira's stall to give him his treats before cleaning Romulus' stall. Zamira devoured the alfalfa treats and nudged my hand for more.

"That's all for now, you big beggar."

I had found Zamira on a website. He was in Kentucky and I fell in love with his photo and had to see him. I made arrangements with the owner and headed to Kentucky with a trailer two days later. It was a long drive but so worth it.

Their trainer walked Zamira out of the barn, saddled and ready for me to 'test drive'. He arched his big, thick neck and side-stepped toward me as if to say, "Here I am! Ride me if you dare." I took the reins from the trainer and cupped my hand over the area above his nostrils. We looked each other in the eye, and I could feel him calm within seconds. We immediately understood each other. I slid onto his back and guided him into the arena. I couldn't believe how smoothly he moved. He had large, dark brown eyes that lured you into his soul.

I took the magnificent animal into the ring and immediately felt his body language change. He began to prance and side-step, nostrils flaring and ears twitching back and forth. I took him around the ring a couple of times in a slow trot to warm him up, then lined him up for a 3-foot jump. He responded to every movement and twitch of my body and paced himself perfectly for the jump. He glided over each jump with such ease and enthusiasm that I knew I had to have this horse! That was a purchase I haven't regretted for a moment.

I grabbed the wheelbarrow, shovel and rake and headed for stall #17. It belonged to Romulus, a 16-hand black Thoroughbred and he belonged to one of my students, Kristin. Romulus is a bit skittish, but a good horse. He had been mishandled at his previous home and Kristin had convinced her parents to rescue him.

Kristin was my second student and had started out by riding my horse Molly, since she didn't have one of her own at that time. Only a month later she found Romulus. They didn't trust each other at first, but Kristin wouldn't give up on him and in a few short months, the two became inseparable. He's a perfect age for a teenager in training – twelve, although he was nine when they brought him to the ranch - and has a heart as big as Texas.

I spent the next hour cleaning his stall and sweeping the aisles between the stalls and indoor arena. I finished and put everything away, flipping off the lights as I left the barn. I started up the hill to the house and was looking forward to a long hot bath, but was stopped in my tracks.

My head began to throb like a bomb was going off. I fell to my knees holding my head, then it stopped and…

"Mandy, can you hear me? It's Jesse. They have had me blocked somehow these past three months. That's why you haven't heard from me but I figured out how to break through the barrier. Oh no, I gotta go! I'll contact you again as soon as I can. Skittles, I love you!"

"What the…?! Jesse?! Who's there? Who the hell is Jesse! Show yourself!" I jumped up and spun in circles looking at the arena, then the barn, toward the house – nothing. I stood there shaking and kept turning in a slow circle. The sun had already slipped behind the hills, so there wasn't much light. Frantic, I started running toward the house. By the time I got to the stairs of the back deck, I was a little dizzy. Holding onto the handrail of the stairs, I walked backward up the four stairs then continued looking toward the barn from the deck. My heart was beating a mile a minute and my hands were shaking.

I hurried into the house and turned on all the lights downstairs. Then I ran upstairs hitting every light switch I passed until I reached the bathroom. I turned on the light. I stood there for a minute and tried to catch my breath. I took a deep breath. My mind must be playing tricks on me. I've been working too much, that had to be it.

I lit two candles and set them on the edge of the bathtub. I turned the hot water faucet on and let it run over my hand. I wasn't paying attention until the heat was too much and snapped me out of my thoughts. I turned on the cold water to balance it out and reached for the light switch that had a dimmer, which enhanced the candles' illumination. I poured some rose-petal bubble bath in the water and slid in. I rested my head on the edge of the tub and let the bubbles and the jets from the tub engulf my entire being. I closed my eyes and tried to clear my head. My whole body and mind eventually relaxed.

I finally got out of the tub when I realized my skin felt like a raisin. I dried off and threw on some sweats. I walked downstairs and made myself a sandwich and grabbed a bag of chips. I decided to eat and watch some television before turning in for the night. The television was on, but I couldn't concentrate on the show, not even sure what show was on. My mind kept turning to Sam then that voice, then Sam again. *Get a grip Mandy!* But telling myself that did not make it happen so I got up and headed to the kitchen.

I put my dishes in the dishwasher, then staggered upstairs to get ready for bed. After brushing my teeth I climbed into the big, comfortable bed and settled under the covers. My thoughts kept going back and forth until I finally drifted off to sleep, and dreams...

> *"Take Tobias around the arena once, then line him up*
> *for the first jump." Sam and Tobias looked magnificent*

together as she got him into a canter. She rounded the first corner of the dressage arena and glanced at me, smiling… she was actually smiling! I was standing in the middle of the arena watching the two of them. I was so proud of her. I looked at the first jump they would take, then turned my head to the hill leading to my house. There he was, standing on the hill waving at me! Waving! As though nothing…no time…no pain had come to me! Just waving like he had gone to the store and wanted me to know he was home. The nerve! I turned my body to face him but he was gone!

"Miss Mandy! Watch out!" I turned back to the arena and Tobias was heading straight toward me! His ears were pinned to his head and his eyes rolled back like a demon horse! I began running but I wasn't fast enough. I turned my head to see where he was, and my face touched his muzzle!

Again, I awoke with a jolt. Sweating, shaking and my jaw hurt from clenching my teeth so hard. I sat up and stared straight ahead for a few minutes trying to figure out this nightmare. This was the second dream in the last couple of months I had had of this man. Who is he? Why did I feel pain when I saw him in my dreams? I needed some serious distractions.

I looked over at the bedside table where my clock radio sat. It read 7:30 a.m. I didn't feel rested at all; how could it be morning already? I crawled out of bed and put on my sweats. I had one class at ten this morning. I convinced myself that this would be a productive day if it killed me. I would make phone calls about Sam, including her case worker and the family court judge. The judge and I were good friends and would have some good advice for me.

I started a pot of coffee and put some raisin bread in the toaster. I wrote a list of things to do while I waited. My mind started to wander in ten different directions…

What am I going to ask the judge? I need to know the exact situation so I better talk to the case worker first. Would I be what Sam needs? What would I do with a teenager full-time? I've never had kids! I would probably screw her up! But she would have a stable home with me. Who is this man that I keep dreaming about? Wait, he said his name is Jesse! Who the hell is Jesse?! He's really cute though. Cute?! Are you nuts?! This is a fantasy man from who knows where...

I blinked hard and snapped my mind out of it. I concentrated on the list and task in front of me. Sam desperately needed my help. This was the distraction I needed.

After I spoke with the case worker, Cheryl, I called the judge. The judge was sympathetic as I hoped and told me to call the foster parents. We were all to meet her in her chambers today at one-thirty. Perfect. I could get through my class, shower and get into town in plenty of time. I didn't want Sam to know what was going on just yet. I needed to wait until I had all my ducks in a row. I asked her foster parents to keep this to themselves for now.

After class I ran into the house to shower and change into more professional-looking clothes. I decided to wear my gray dress. It was light gray, long with a black belt. It had a V-neck, so I put on a thin gold chain and my small gold horse-head earrings. I slipped on my black flats, grabbed my purse and ran downstairs.

It was only eleven-thirty, which gave me plenty of time to get some lunch in town before meeting with the judge. I hopped into my truck and called Becca.

"Hey, can you meet me for lunch at Billy's Café?"

"Sure. Is everything ok, you sound frantic?" Leave it to Becca to notice what I tried to hide.

"By this afternoon I'm hoping to be great. I'll tell you all about it at lunch."

I explained the situation with Sam but not the dream. I decided to leave that craziness to myself.

"Wow! That's fantastic Mandy! Sam will be so happy! Can I come to the court house with you?"

"Absolutely! I wasn't sure if I would ask you but I could use the moral support."

"Of course I want to be there!" She hugged me then we walked out to our cars.

Becca stayed in the hallway while we met with the judge in her chambers. Judge Hathaway was a very fair and empathetic judge who cared deeply about every child that entered her courtroom. I had been before her as a social worker and she seemed to respect my input. I explained the amount of room in my house and that it's only me living there. There was a school bus that could stop at the end of my road to take her to school every day. She was halfway through her junior year, so only needed foster parents for a year and a half. I felt I could provide a stable – no pun intended – secure environment for her. Sam knew the ranch inside and out and would be a tremendous help while continuing her education.

Cheryl had absolutely no objection and had been to my ranch a couple of times for social visits. She had known me for years and agreed that Sam would thrive living with me on the ranch. The foster parents were thrilled at the idea, as they could continue having contact with Sam. They too had become attached to this bright young girl.

"Well, I don't need to think about this any further. Everyone seems to agree that it's in Sam's best interest to live with you, Mandy. I have no objections. Please do not hesitate to call me and send me updates. Cheryl, take care of the paperwork and it will be a done deal." She shook all our hands and we left her chambers.

Becca could tell immediately and let out a happy scream, then turned every shade of red when she realized how loud she'd been. We all laughed.

"Mandy, I will get the I's dotted and T's crossed, then call you tomorrow morning." Cheryl shook my hand and motioned for the foster parents to follow her. I shook their hands, but the foster mom, Carolyn, wouldn't have anything to do with that. She pulled me into a hug. "Thank you, Mandy. I know Sam will be in good hands and will be so happy."

"Carolyn, I think I need her more than she needs me. Call me when you're finished at Cheryl's office and we'll tell Sam together." She nodded and left with her husband and Cheryl.

"I'm so happy Mandy!" Becca gave me a big hug and we parted ways. I got back to the ranch and decided to check on Tony and the horses before heading up to the house.

"Hi, Mandy. What happened with the judge?"

"Hi Tony – well, I'm going to have a guest for about a year and a half!"

"Wow! That's excellent! Congratulations!" He gave me a bear hug, and I could tell he was genuinely excited.

"Sam's a cool kid and she's lucky to have you in her life."

"Thanks. How are the other kids?"

He laughed, knowing I was referring to the horses. "They're good. I've got Tobias and Molly out in the pasture. I was about to go get them."

"Okay. I think I'll try to make some calls for the show. I'll try to ease the next meltdown from Becca."

"I would really appreciate that, since her meltdowns don't end here. They carry on at home." He smiled and turned toward the pasture.

The two of them bicker like cats and dogs but it's funny fighting, never mean or hurtful.

I got to my desk and pulled out Becca's file with the show information. Amazingly, I sat for two hours without my mind wandering and tackled all the lingering problems. I was able to pin down the food vendors; the ribbon company assured me they would be ready by next Tuesday, and I got hold of three judges. Done!

The only thing left to do was the ambulance. I called the chief and explained we couldn't begin the show until the ambulance was in place. He assured me that they would do their best. I decided that thirty minutes wouldn't be too bad and hopefully we could stall that long without too many frustrations.

The next day was a great one. Becca was thrilled that everything was done for the show then Cheryl called and said all the paperwork was done and Sam could move in any time! I called Carolyn and we decided to meet for lunch at 1:00 today to spring the good news on Sam.

I arrived at the café about 12:45 and grabbed a booth. The waitress had just set my glass of tea on the table when Carolyn, her husband Mike, and Sam walked in. As tough as it was, they had not said a word to Sam to spoil the surprise. She had no idea why we were all meeting. I got up to greet them.

"Hi, how are you?" I shook Mike and Carolyn's hands. I winked at Sam as we all sat down.

"Ok, just say it and get it over with." Sam was still standing and getting agitated. I knew we better tell her quick.

"Sit down Sam. Mandy has some great news." Carolyn said as she motioned for Sam to sit next to me.

"Well, you won't be able to stay with Miss Carolyn or Mike any longer." I had turned sideways to face her in the booth. Sam's head lowered and she started twirling her napkin. I was about to open my mouth again when the waitress appeared.

"What can I get you three to drink?" She asked while laying down three more menus. I waited for them to order and the waitress to leave before continuing.

"You can't live there any longer - but you can live with me until you graduate high school, even longer if you want!" Sam sat there for a few seconds still staring at her napkin. Then she turned her head to me and looked at my face. I could tell she was attempting to read my expression and see if I was pulling her leg.

"Are you serious?! The case worker went for that?!"

"Yes she did and the judge was thrilled. Sam it's official, you're going to live with me!" Sam was so happy that she nearly knocked over our table when she reached over to give me a hug. She blushed, then slowly rose and gave Carolyn and Mike a hug.

"Mike and Carolyn can come out to the ranch any time, and you can have all the contact with them you want." I said as Sam sat back down. She couldn't hold back the tears, as hard as she tried.

"Thank you so much!" She put her arms on the table to touch all our hands. Her amber eyes watered, but they were happy tears.

"I should be thanking you! You have no idea how great this will be for me as well."

We finished eating and decided she would move in this Saturday. We also decided to skip the extra riding time Friday so she could pack. We said our good-byes and I spent the rest of the afternoon shopping for Sam. I had a lot to do to prepare her room before Saturday.

The room I designated for Sam was furnished for the most part with a queen-sized bed; chest of drawers, dresser with mirror; desk, and bedside table. I wanted to add a few little touches I hoped would be inviting for a teen. I figured if she needed or wanted anything else, we could go shopping this weekend.

Saturday came without a hitch. Sam, Carolyn and Mike showed up at the ranch about eleven a.m. Mike took her suitcase, duffel bag and backpack up to her room. We girls stood in the kitchen discussing how excited she was to be moving in. I asked if they would like to stay for lunch, but Mike and Carolyn declined and said they needed to get home. The three of them hugged and cried.

"I'll see you all the time." Sam said as she gave Carolyn a very tight hug.

"I know, Honey. You call me whenever you want. I love you very much. You be a big help around here." Carolyn pulled back but kept her hands on Sam's shoulders.

"I will, and I love you guys too. Thank you for everything you've done for me." She leaned over to Mike.

"It was always a pleasure. I love you too, Sam," Mike whispered as he gave her a hug. They left and Sam and I stood on the front porch for a moment trying to collect ourselves.

"Well, I hope you like spaghetti and garlic bread. I'm not much of a cook, but I can fix sauce out of a jar with the best of them."

"I love spaghetti and jar sauce. I like just about anything."

"Then we'll get along just fine. Why don't you go check out your room and make a list of things you need, and we'll go shopping this afternoon."

"Cool." Sam ran upstairs and I proceeded into the kitchen to try to be domestic.

After lunch we went to town and shopped til we dropped then headed back to the ranch. We had picked up a movie and pizza and decided that would be our evening.

About 11:30 we were both exhausted and ready for bed. I fell into bed and, after the exciting week that had just passed it didn't take long to fall fast asleep…

Sam came bounding down the stairs dressed and ready for school. I handed her some money for lunch and she ran out the door to catch the bus. I watched from the front door. I felt like she was my daughter on her first day of kindergarten. I felt so calm and content as I watched the yellow bus pull up to whisk her off. I started to go back into the house when I spotted something across the road at the edge of my neighbor's pasture. I squinted and stared, thinking it must be something reflecting in the sun. There were two small red lights — or were they eyes? — in the tall grass. They seemed to blink, because for a split second they disappeared and then reappeared, and just stared at me. Actually, it looked like two sets of lights or eyes, whatever they were. A cougar maybe? They don't usually come this close to civilization and stay higher up the mountain.

I got a creepy feeling and wanted to slam the door and lock it, but I couldn't move. If they were eyes, we were staring at each other! I finally backed up into the house, not taking my eyes off those glowing spots.

All of a sudden I was in the kitchen staring out the French doors toward the barn. How did I move through the house so fast?

"Mandy. It's Jesse. Turn around, and please don't be afraid." The voice was whispering. I stood frozen and did not turn around. I concentrated on the barn. The voice continued in a whisper…

"I found out what he did to you, and I just have to get through to you before he figures out I'm here. You have to remember me - remember us. Please. He couldn't have erased us from your memory forever! It has to be there somewhere." Just then my blood turned cold. A second voice sounded that was not a whisper.

"Jesse, give it up! Her memory of you is gone and will never come back!"

I screamed "Leave me alone!!" I tried to escape though the French doors, but they wouldn't open. I tried to wake myself up.

"That's right, Mandy, wake up and forget this dream." This voice, the second one, was creepy almost evil sounding.

"NO! Leave her alone! Mandy, it's Jesse! Don't wake up yet! Don't listen to him! Remember us, remember you and me! You nicknamed me 'Scooby' and I nicknamed you 'Skittles'. Think! I know you can remember."

I needed to wake up, get back to reality, change dreams, or whatever it would take. I felt a hand on my shoulder that sent a chill down my spine. My eyes were clenched shut but I turned to see who it was. I slowly opened them and gazed into the most beautiful blue eyes I'd ever seen. It was the same man I had seen in the other dream and on the hill when I was awake. He was a gorgeous vision and when I looked into those mesmerizing eyes I felt serene again – familiar. Why? I have never seen *him before! Just as I was about to ask him that question, he was snatched up and thrown across the room!*

I screamed and backed closer to the doors.

The man stood up from across the room and looked at me. There was fear in his eyes, but I didn't feel he was frightened for himself.

"Mandy, it's okay. I'll try again later. Wake up! I don't want you to see any more of this. Wake up!"

"No, Mandy. You need to see him get his ass kicked!" Again, the evil voice!

"Mandy, WAKE UP! I love you and I'll see you soon"…

My eyes flew open. I should have been terrified, but instead I felt calm, almost relieved and excited. But why??

Chapter 4

The Island

"Oh my God!"

"What?!"

"The island! We're back on the island!"

We broke through some thick trees and were flying about ten feet off the ground. I thought for sure we were going to hit a tree head-on. The creature flew in and out and around trees with such grace and so fast! Obviously used to these daredevil acrobatics. Without any warning, it dropped us and we landed with a hard jolt in a clearing near the trees.

It was a small clearing surrounded by heavy foliage. We both stood and checked each other for any injuries.

"Hello Mr. Damien, welcome back. We been expecting you." His English wasn't the best but understandable. He was a little guy, Indian maybe? Damien bowed his head slightly and shook his hand. A noise behind us interrupted the reunion. We whipped around, and there again were the crimson eyes! All six of our eyes stared at each other, not moving or breathing.

It stepped out of the foliage. It wasn't the creature that brought us here, but it was the same eyes that kept peering at us over the last few days. As its body emerged further into the clearing I was in utter shock! It showed its body this time, and it was gigantic! As it came toward us, Damien and I took a few steps back but bumped into something. We turned around and saw the creature that had brought us here. It stood almost as tall as the pine trees and looked like a giant owl – but evil. He had the head of an owl but the body looked more like an eagle. It must have a five story wing span and its talons had to be ten feet long! Those are what held us in the air?! How are we still alive?! All I knew for sure, this thing was huge and ugly!

We turned back around to the other creature. It was a black panther, but colossal in size, as huge as five grizzlies combined. It was massive, but beautiful and terrifying at the same time. Its coat looked like silk and its sheen nearly blinded us. Its eyes were piercing and mesmerizing. Its chest must be five to six feet wide, and the muscles on its shoulders rippled all the way down to its huge paws. Its mouth was slightly open. Its teeth were ivory and the tongue was pink. A drop of drool fell to the ground. All three of us just stood our own ground and stared each other down.

Then it morphed. It actually morphed! I felt like I was in a B-rated horror movie! Its body went from a black, gleaming and blinding beauty to a distortion that was indescribable. We were like deer in the headlights; we couldn't move or breathe. It stood on its hind legs as it was changing, and its feet became male humanoid feet, and the legs and torso slowly became a human male. His head remained that of a panther til the last; a giant black panther head on top of a normal, human body. "Normal" – what a joke! Nothing about my life over the past few days has been normal! It was as if the creature was toying with us and kept his head a secret. It remained part human and part panther. The suspense must have been too much for him, however, and the head began to morph into a human head. As it formed and became human, Damien and I grabbed each other's shoulders.

"What the..? How on earth...?!" Damien stammered, as I felt his shoulder muscles go limp, and he nearly fell to the ground. I grabbed him under the arm and pulled him to his feet, not taking my eyes off the – creature...human – I didn't know what it was.

The three of us stood there staring at each other for a few moments longer. Then "it" spoke:

"Hi there, brothers! I've been waiting years for this moment and finally – all three of us are reunited…well, united. Damien, it took you long enough to find Jesse. I thought you'd never figure things out. You drove me crazy! I gave you hint after hint and still, nothing. But with a little push from me, here we all are. Isn't it wonderful?!" He rolled his eyes, and suddenly a little person ran up to him with clothes. He put them on then continued…

"Where are my manners? Let me introduce myself. I am your brother, Nikias, your identical triplet as you can see. This fine-feathered friend behind you is Buzzard. He was our transportation to Paradise. Yes, I was with you the whole time on his back. I got to ride first class. I don't like coach, it hurts. Oh, and Jesse we are Jaguars, not panthers. They may be the same thing but Jaguar is much cooler." He spoke in a condescending tone that made me want to punch him, hard.

We stood there frozen. I couldn't move or utter a sound. My jaw was locked in the open position.

"Aw c'mon, boys. Cat got your tongues? Pun intended, by the way. Well I guess I know who got the funny gene from our dysfunctional gene pool. Let me give you a hint – it's not you two." Nikias circled us as we stood cemented in place. It seemed as if we were being assessed as a menu item. Nikias finally stopped circling and faced us, standing a couple of feet away.

"You know, when I changed into my handsome human form I actually did that much more slowly than I normally do, for your benefit. I wanted to keep you in suspense for as long as possible. I usually phase in the blink of an eye. Want to see?" Without giving us a chance to respond, in less than an eye-blink he indeed "phased" into the gigantic Jaguar creature. The shredded clothes he had just put on fell to the ground. His head alone was the size of my entire body and then some. His eyes were crimson, blood red. He towered over Damien and me, staring a hole right through us.

Damien was finally able to utter: "This...this can't be. I mean... what the...who, what are..."

Nikias quickly phased back into human form so he could speak. A different little person, Indian or whatever immediately rushed over to him with another pair of shorts. These poor guys must keep an endless supply of clothes for him and work in shifs.

"Oh for cryin' out loud! Spit it out! Who and what am I? Well – I am your missing link, your brother! Personally, I think it's a waste of time bringing you two here. I can handle the situation but NO, they don't agree. Whatever! They think it's going to take an army of us." This strange maniac was pacing back and forth in front of us while he ranted.

"So I have to give you a synopsis of our kind. It's going to be quick so pay attention! We can turn into a Jaguars; read minds; speak to anyone with our minds; plant visions and dreams into peoples' heads. Ooh, and go into peoples' dreams which is a real mind game. We can find anyone by picturing their face; become invisible; make people or creatures implode, literally and that, by the way, is a very cool talent. It's a little messy but effective. We also have a really keen sense of vision and hearing.

Of course, you two have already experienced most of the abilities but you're amateurs and don't know how to handle them. Damien, you would've been a lot further along if you would have stuck around a little longer in paradise. But they decided we needed to find Jesse and I wanted you to do it. I just didn't realize how long it would take you to figure out your mission.

But whatever, you guys will have formal training soon enough. Of course, all the training in the world won't make you two as good as me." He turned to me. "And Jesse, *your* education is just beginning." Nikias took a deep breath and wheeled around to face the crowd of little people that had emerged during his ranting. He spoke to them in their language. The chief nodded his head, took a couple of steps backward and turned to the others. They all walked away, leaving us standing in the clearing.

Nikias turned back to Damien and me and winked.

"They're a little afraid of me. I don't get it – I'm such a nice guy." He laughed at himself, then stepped between Damien and me and put his arms around our shoulders.

"We are gonna have some fun in the months and years – well – eternity together. Oh, did I forget to mention that? We don't die. Ever. We're immortal! Isn't that a hoot?! And if we are shot, stabbed – even blown up – we heal. No dagger through the heart, kryptonite, silver bullet, not even fire. We are 'fire resistant'!" He chuckled. "Well, I suppose there is one way but I will never be the one to tell you that neat little secret."

"Now here's the tricky part. I was 'changed' three years ago, which is when my immortality began. So I stopped aging at the ripe ol' age of twenty-two. Damien, you were changed a year ago, so you stopped aging at twenty-four. Poor Jesse is the old man of the three of us at twenty-five." He stopped talking and took another deep breath, but it didn't take long for him to continue. I think he enjoyed hearing his own voice.

"Damien, I could've saved your sorry butt sooner but we needed Jesse, and I wanted you to change him. I was mad as hell when TJ turned on us, but it actually worked out beautifully. I knew you still loved that girl – Cassie – and when that idiot kidnapped her I nearly killed him, but I wanted to see how it would play out. Your weakness for Cassie forced you to take desperate measures." He grinned and said "you did exactly as I hoped – changed our brother." Nikias took his arms from around our shoulders and dropped them to his sides. He walked forward a couple of steps and turned to face us. We stood staring at him, and he looked back and forth between Damien and me.

Then Damien seemed to snap out of his trance and confronted Nikias. He walked the three paces to our 'brother' and stood merely inches from Nikias' face. "What in the hell are you talking about? Who are you really, and why do you look like us? Plastic surgery? Why? I know we don't have another brother. I heard our bastard of a father tell the story to that idiot friend of his. Why would he lie to him? He was confessing while he was in a drunken stupor. Tell me what's going on, right now!" Damien took another step closer, but Nikias stood his ground and didn't budge. I started to feel a little nervous for Damien, thinking of the gigantic creature this maniac was able to morph into.

Nikias' eyes began to change into the crimson red, and I knew this was it. He was going to turn Damien into soup all over the ground. Damien still did not move – he didn't seem to be breathing. All of a sudden Nikias' body language relaxed. His eyes returned to normal, and he burst into genuine laughter. He laughed uncontrollably until his eyes watered and his face turned red. Damien took a few steps back toward me. *Oh sure, now you back off, D! Seeing him almost morph into a monster didn't worry you, but laughing does? Are you nuts?!*

Hey! I can hear you guys. Remember, I have the same powers as both of you, except mine are more…well, experienced. Nikias stopped laughing as he spoke to us in his head. His body language returned to the tense and cocky version again as he stepped toward us. "I may not be able to kill you any longer, but I can bring you to your knees in excruciating pain for a short time. Don't you EVER demand anything from me again!" His face was an inch from Damien's. Damien stood firm and didn't waver. They each stood their ground, fists clenched at their sides.

C'mon Damien, you're almost there. DO IT!! Nikias was taunting Damien, and I couldn't figure out what was going on. Did he want him to hit him? I could see Damien getting more enraged by the second, yet he still didn't move. His breathing became uneven and louder, but still he didn't budge. Nikias was trying to get him to do something – but what? Suddenly I wished I hadn't wondered.

Damien, you have no idea how many times I thought of entering Cassie's cage while she was being held captive and…hmmm, you can use your imagination on that one. Nikias jumped back a good five feet, and what happened next seemed to surprise him. I could see Damien's muscles tense under his t-shirt; his jaw muscles quivered and clenched tightly. I couldn't see his face, but I knew it was changing with the rest of his body. I stood only three feet or so from him. *Jesse, you might want to stand back. You don't want to be in Damien's way.*

"Nikias, what have you done? What is going on with Damien? Damien!" He wasn't listening. "Nikias, ANSWER ME!" Both of them ignored me. I hadn't known Damien long but I felt very protective of him all of a sudden.

I stepped back a few feet, yet my gut was telling me to grab Damien, run through the forest, find the ocean and swim, just swim until we can't see this damned island. My mind raced through all kinds of scenarios as I watched Damien. I tried to get into his head, but it was a raging tornado in there. Suddenly his body started swelling...actually – swelling! I couldn't take it any longer; a normal person would have seen that his brother was in danger, grab him and RUN.

The concern and fear for Damien suddenly turned to rage - real spine-tingling, blood-boiling rage. I guess I had jumped in front of Damien to protect him from Nikias, but in the process I morphed – phased – or whatever the scientific term may be. I didn't feel anything when it happened but the rage I felt was unlike any emotion I had ever felt before. I couldn't speak except to make a low growl, so I had to communicate with my mind.

Damien GET THE HELL OUT OF HERE! What I didn't know was that human forms couldn't hear me.

He can't hear you bro! But look at you!! I didn't realize what a show off you are. Nikias had phased the instant I did.

Shut up! I've had it with your head games. Just let us go! If I never see you again it'll be too soon. We stood faced to face, squaring off.

Get over yourself, Jesse! We are done for now and going home to eat. Neither of you is going anywhere! Now either try to take me or turn back into your human form. I wanted to rip his big black head off his shoulders. I turned to look at Damien. His rage had dissipated, and he stood there staring, his mouth wide open disbelief. I felt my body relax, I think more for Damien's sake than mine, I became myself again – Jesse. Nikias had also morphed back to human form. He jogged over to a huge boulder that stood at the edge of the clearing and returned with shorts and t-shirts for us. *He must keep clothes all over this island.*

I said, "Damien, you okay?"

"You and Nikias almost killed each other, and you're asking me if I'm okay?!"

"Well, yeah."

"I'm fine. What about you??"

"Oh, this is so touching – but this little love-fest is over. Let's go, I need food." Nikias began walking toward the forest.

"Whatever – let's go." I grabbed Damien's arm and pulled him forward. We caught up with Nikias quickly. My curiosity got the better of me.

"Where do all the clothes come from?" Damien seemed to be more relaxed but I could tell he had as many questions as I did. Where the clothes come from was the least of my curiosity.

"We have 'helpers' with an endless supply of them." Nikias replied. He then turned his attention to me.

"I thought Damien would be the most natural at phasing since he has had the other abilities longer. But I guess I'm allowed to be wrong once. Now, that's enough for one day. Let's get home and have dinner. I might do a question and answer session for you after we eat but you better make the questions good ones. I do get bored easily, as you will quickly learn." He laughed as he turned toward the forest and began walking. Damien and I stood there staring at each other for a moment then followed our so-called brother.

We walked deeper into the forest. The foliage and trees were so thick and the air was heavy. The sunlight disappeared and it was very difficult to see where we were walking. Both Damien and I kept tripping over large tree roots and rocks. Nikias proceeded effortlessly through the thick forest. The further we walked the more it felt like we were being watched. Maybe it was one of the 'little helpers' Nikias told us about. I wasn't sure if he meant one of the tribesmen or if there were other 'helpers'.

Damien, does any of this look familiar?

I can't tell. When I would go exploring it all looked exactly the same and the night I escaped it was very dark. I was very lucky to find my way to the boat.

Nikias jerked to a stop, and Damien almost ran into him. He turned to look at us, but his eyes were that crimson color.

"Are you freakin' kidding me? Have you not learned anything yet?!" He took a very deep breath, and his eyes returned to our family's baby blue color. "You did NOT escape. We let you go, as we needed you to start the process – the process of finding Jesse. And for the last time, QUIT using your inside voices! I know it's still new and exciting for you Jesse, but it drives me crazy!" He turned and began walking again.

We hadn't taken more than three steps when Damien stopped suddenly and I smacked into him. "Wait a minute. Nikias, you said 'we let you go'. Who is 'we'? Who else is here besides the tribespeople? What do they have to do with all of us?"

"I told you, the question and answer session will be after dinner. I'm starving and you don't want me getting so hungry that you two start looking like a couple of turkey breasts. I could very quickly turn have dinner right here and now." He grinned. "I will tell you that when we're in that body, we have the same instincts as all other wild cats, to an extent. We still have the reasoning and human thought process, but it's very easy to get distracted while in that form." Nikias never missed a beat walking and talking and was far ahead of us. We started walking again but nearly had to run to catch up.

The rest of the journey was in silence except for the snapping of branches and twigs, and our tripping over tree roots. I couldn't keep my mind off Mandy, and worried that something had happened to the girls after we were abducted. I tried 'contacting' her but was rudely interrupted.

"Mandy…Mandy, can you hear me?"

"Knock it off! You keep forgetting that I can hear you, Big Brother."

"Look, I just want to know that they're safe and when we'll see them again." The more I thought and 'spoke' of Mandy, the angrier I became.

The girls are fine. So, shut up and walk.

There was no way to judge how far or how long we had walked. I knew it was daylight when we left the clearing, but couldn't tell if it was light or dark now, as the forest was so thick and ominous. Finally, we broke out of the forest and the view before us was spectacular!

Damien and I stood there in awe. Nikias strutted ahead of us, oblivious to the fact that his two newfound brothers were not behind him.

"What the…" Damien stammered.

"This doesn't look familiar? You weren't here the last time?"

"No. I have no idea where we are." Damien took a step forward toward Nikias, but I stayed put. I stared at the view, not paying attention to my brothers. Brothers?! I still felt as though I might eventually wake up and this would all be a bizarre dream. Beyond the edge of the clearing was a small, serene lake, surrounded by a rocky half-circle of mountain, perhaps thirty stories high. Right in the center was a large waterfall, cascading down off the mountain. The scene was breathtaking.

"Jesse! Hurry up, we don't have all day! Believe me, I will have you for lunch if you don't get a move on!" Nikias yelled at me from the edge of the lake, a few hundred yards away. Damien had just reached him.

I jogged up to meet them. "Nikias, where the hell are you taking us? I want to get back to my own life…NOW!"

Nikias turned to me and his eyes had changed. He spoke in a quiet, calm voice: "Jesse, I have told you that the question and answer session will be after we eat. If I have to tell you again…well, let's just say that you will be in some extraordinary pain."

"Fine! Let's get this over with."

The three of us stood at the edge of the water for a couple of minutes, staring at the rock formation and the waterfall. Nikias started stomping his foot on a patch of grass. I assumed it was because he was agitated and anxious; but he didn't move from the small patch of grass. Suddenly a thundering, ear-splitting sound came from behind the waterfall! The water stopped! It just stopped! It was as if someone had turned off a faucet.

"Finally! They must have been sleeping." Nikias began to pace back and forth while Damien and I just stood there, dumfounded. The rock formation, where the waterfall had been, began to open like a gigantic garage door! I guessed that was the thundering noise. A red speedboat suddenly burst out of the mountain and to the edge of the lake, where we stood. Quickly it turned sideways, splashing water on us as it came to a stop.

"Knock it off!" Nikias grabbed the side of the boat and pulled it toward him as if it were a toy. The driver of the boat was a male Caucasian, approximately 5' 9", with light brown hair, slender and with blue eyes. He didn't say a word as he extended his hand to Nikias, who jumped in and glared at the two of us. I decided not to argue or cause any further aggravation until Nikias had something of substance in his stomach. Damien and I jumped into the boat then it sped across the lake toward the enormous open doorway. As the door loomed closer, I felt a large knot growing in the pit of my stomach.

From a distance the area behind the door looked pitch-black. As we came closer I could see a small amount of light, but couldn't make out its source. The boat slowed and eventually came to a stop, inside the mountain! The driver turned off the engine and the boat glided up to a short pier just inside the entry, which led to a flat rock surface. The lighting was very dim, so I could only see about ten feet in front of us.

The driver jumped out and once again extended his hand to Nikias, who abruptly grabbed it and pulled himself out of the boat. He nearly knocked the driver back inside the boat. Then they both turned and started walking. Damien and I looked at each other, shrugged, climbed from the boat and followed.

Damien sped up a little to catch up with the others, but I lingered behind, taking in the surroundings. It was very dark and musty. I figured that was to be expected when one is inside a mountain.

I caught up to the other three and we continued a few hundred feet further, when Nikias and the driver stopped. It had gotten darker the further we walked, but there were small lights on the ceiling of the cave which illuminated our way ever so slightly. When they stopped, Damien and I looked at each other and then at Nikias. I was about to open my mouth and ask why we stopped, when Nikias reached out with his right hand and pushed a flat spot on the wall of the cave. Part of the wall in front of us suddenly became a doorway and opened. Of course it did. The way the past few weeks have gone, it wouldn't have surprised me to see Alice in Wonderland on the other side. Why not? Most of what has happened has been bizarre, weird, mystical, or just plain freaky.

The doorway was an area just large enough for one of us to fit through at a time. Nikias led the way, followed by the driver, then Damien, and I was last to hunch over and squeeze through. When I got through the doorway and stood upright, Damien was in front of me frozen in his tracks. I quickly glanced in the direction of his gaze and my jaw dropped. A small city emerged before us. My gaze wandered to the left and right, up and down. All around us and on every square inch of mountain wall were signs of life. The walls had what looked like small caves with balconies at the openings. I assumed the caves housed families. I couldn't count how many there were. There were people standing on some of the balconies, staring at the newcomers. Flower pots decorated most of the balconies, and I estimated there were at least five hundred mini-caves within this gigantic one. Awesome!

I wondered how the families got up and down, and that question was quickly answered. To our right I heard a strange whooshing sound. A long rope ladder that looked like it was made from sturdy vine material tumbled down from one of the caves. A child about nine years old bounded down the ladder, skipping the last six rungs. He landed with an excited thump and sprinted toward us. Nikias and the driver had disappeared, which was something I was getting used to.

"Your brother is over here." The child took my hand and pulled me forward at a run – well, he jogged and Damien and I did a fast-walk. I looked down at our path, which was a light beige cobblestone. As we stepped onto the flat surface, I noticed about thirty small brick homes scattered around. People had started to gather outside their homes and on the balconies to gawk at us. In front of us, at the end of the cobblestone path, was a large two-story brick home. It kind of reminded me of my house in Boulder, but with an extra floor.

The slender young boy stopped in front of the house and looked at me. His eyes were light brown and full of questions, but also fear, as he looked back at the house.

"How did you know he was our brother?" I asked.

"Duh! Look at the three of you. It's so cool! I wish I had a twin or triplet!" He let go of my hand and ran back to his house, or rather his cave.

Damien and I stood outside the two-story house.

Wow, they really do look like Nikias!

I hope they're nicer than he is.

This is really getting creepy.

Great – two more spoiled brats we have to take care of.

I had let my guard down and started 'hearing' the thoughts of some of the townspeople, or whatever they're called. 'Cave people?' That doesn't sound psychotic!

"Hurry up, you two! I swear, I'm going to die of starvation before you make it through the front door!" Nikias was using his 'inside' voice, which made me wonder if these people know what we can do? Hell, *I* don't even know what we can do!

"Okay, okay! Sheesh, we're coming!" Damien and I walked up the three steps leading to the porch and front door. Nikias stood inside the door watching us. Damien stepped inside first and I was right behind him, but suddenly I couldn't move. I was half in and half out when a tingling sensation started in my face and ran down my entire body. I wasn't in pain, but couldn't move.

The other two were oblivious to all of this and continued through the house. The feeling finally subsided after a few long seconds, so I moved on. Inside the front door was a small foyer with a high ceiling. A crystal chandelier hung from the ceiling with reflections of light bouncing off the walls. A staircase leading upward stood directly in front of the door, and two rooms lay to the right and left. The room on the right looked to be a library or den and the room on the left maybe a family room.

I walked down the hallway to the left of the staircase, assuming that led to the back of the house where the kitchen and dining area would be. I was correct, and it was no surprise that Nikias was already eating. He sat at a large oak dining table stuffing his face. Off to the right were two swinging doors that must lead to the kitchen.

"Well, hi Grandpa. It's about time you showed up. Sit down and eat – or not. I really don't care." Nikias had a mouthful of chicken when he spoke, and continued shoving food into his mouth. Damien sat in one of the six chairs that surrounded the table, and of course Nikias sat at the head of the table. Three plates of food had been placed on the table, and mine sat next to Damien.

I stood there for a few moments, staring at Nikias. *How can he possibly be related to us? He's a jerk! Rude, condescending asshole!*

"Well, I feel the same way about you, big brother. You keep forgetting that we can all hear each other, spoken words or not. Sit, eat! You're getting on my nerves standing there." He looked at Damien, who was picking at his food. Nikias glared at him, then continued shoveling food into his mouth. I sat next to Damien and began to eat. It was actually delicious: fried chicken, mashed potatoes with butter and sour cream, rolls, and corn on the cob. In the middle of the table sat a large apple pie and three dishes of vanilla ice cream.

Damien had been thinking of the girls and his journal. I caught bits and pieces of his thoughts. I tried not to 'invade' his privacy, but Nikias didn't care and plowed through his thoughts.

Relax Damien, the girls are fine. In fact, Mandy had the bright idea of going to your house to find your journals. She and Cassie are attempting to find you two. Bless their little hearts, they won't be able to. I have blocked you two from seeing the girls so I can keep watch. You two have enough to worry about without the distractions. If I have to put up with you then I'm going to have some fun. The elders say we need your help, whatever! He laughed out loud and polished off the rest of his dinner. After he finished, he raised his right arm and snapped his fingers in the air. A short, round gentleman came bursting through the swinging door to Nikias' side. "Yes sir?"

"Seconds please." The man abruptly spun around and disappeared into the kitchen. Damien and I stared at Nikias after the man left, disgusted. My blood was already boiling and my stomach was churning when he had spoken of the girls. He didn't deserve to speak of them, let alone 'watch' them!

"What?! I said please."

My jaw began to ache and I realized I had been clenching my teeth. I kept picturing him 'watching' Mandy. I wanted to reach over, grab him by the neck and squeeze until his eyes popped out.

I didn't care that he was my newfound family member; he was the type you love to hate.

Such vivid images, Brother! Maybe we should take this out to a more appropriate venue and see what you've got. You fascinated me with the speed of your first phasing. I can feel your rage right now through my veins. I love it! Do you want me to show you a preview of your sweet Mandy? The way she is frantically going through Damien's journals is priceless. She wants to find her beloved Jesse with everything she has. It's heartbreaking, really. He chuckled.

As Nikias continued 'speaking' to me, I felt like I was going to explode – it was like lava about to erupt from a volcano. I knew I needed to calm down, as I didn't want to give him the satisfaction of getting a rise out of me. So I looked away and concentrated on Damien. Then I pictured a giant black hole and kept that image in my head, hoping to block Nikias out.

Damien blurted "What is with you two? Nikias, I'm about to reach over and knock you on your ass! I know you were 'speaking' to Jesse, but how did you block me out so only Jesse could hear you? I can feel how furious Jesse is and it's really pissing me off!" He glared at Nikias, who didn't seem at all concerned and kept his attention on me, which angered me further.

I had been out of control with my emotions. Being a cop for so many years had given me thick skin. I had learned to let comments from perps roll off me and ignore their crazy rants. But Nikias had a way of getting under my skin and burrowing deep. He knew Mandy was my Achilles heel, and he was obviously going to use that to the fullest. I had to get my emotions and rage in check, so I tried to keep my thoughts inside the black hole I had imagined.

"Really Jesse? Are you serious? You think picturing this black hole is keeping me out?! You crack me up…for that matter, I crack myself up!" He laughed again. "I have to admit that you are going to be easier to train than I thought, and you are a natural at this. But you are absolutely no match for me, and you need to learn not to wear your heart on your sleeve." Having said that, Nikias stood up, knocking his chair backward. The chair crashed to the floor. I grabbed the edge of the table and held on, never taking my eyes off Nikias. I could feel the lava begin to churn inside me. He walked to other side of the table across from me and grabbed his side. I tried to pull the table away from him, but he retained his iron grip. The pressure of us playing tug-of-war with this beautiful table weakened it broke in half! Poor Damien had food and water all over him as the dishes had slid to either side of the table. Nikias didn't break a sweat and his attention stayed riveted on me.

He continued to stare me up and down. There were absolutely no thoughts running through either of our minds – just colors… first red, then black, continuously switching back and forth. I had never wanted another human being dead before, but Nikias had changed that for me. I hated him for that as well.

We stood there for what seemed like hours and I could feel what he felt; see what he saw; well, except for the girls. He was able to let me 'see' only what he wanted me to see. The red and black in my mind swirled faster and faster, until…everything stopped. What was left was an image of two giant Jaguars in battle, and I assumed that was Nikias' cocky way of challenging me to a fight.

"Done! Let's go NOW, Nikias!" I threw my half of the broken table across the room. Damien, still sitting in his chair, now without a table in front of him and soaked with food and water, stared at me. I could feel him trying to 'get in'. I wanted to protect him so I blocked him. It didn't occur to me until later to question how I was able to do that. It just happened, I blocked Damien out of my head. Why couldn't I keep the other S.O.B. brother out of my head? I would figure out a way to do it if it killed me, and even Nikias wouldn't see it coming.

Then, Nikias allowed me to see an image of the clearing we had abandoned earlier to feed his stomach. My eyes had been closed most of this time to help keep Damien out, but when I realized where our battle would take place, my eyes popped open.

Nikias was gone. I looked down at Damien. He sat motionless and quiet; when he did speak, it was barely a whisper.

"He just...vanished. I was looking at him and all he did was stare at you. I looked back at you and out of the corner of my eye I saw a flash, I think, and he was gone. Just gone." Damien seemed to be in a trance. I couldn't tell if he was confused or if Nikias had played mind games with him. It didn't matter, I was going to do damage to that cocky, arrogant, self-centered, look-alike maniac!

"Damien, stay here and I'll be back later."

"You're crazy if you think you're leaving without me! You may have kept me out of your heads earlier, but I know what you two are about to do. I'm going with you!"

"Ugh! Fine, let's go."

It didn't take long to find the clearing, which amazed me since I'd had no clue earlier where we were. The other strange thing was that I could smell Nikias! That creeped me out but I kept pushing forward, following the scent. We rounded a small turn in the path, I moved some foliage out of the way, and there it was.

This time I actually convinced Damien to stay put just inside the forest's edge. I didn't have time to ask what was wrong, but there was fear in his eyes. I would find out later – but right now, it was time to put Nikias in his place, preferably six feet under.

"I heard that, Jesse!"

Where was he? I closed my eyes and repositioned myself to face the crunching sound of a breaking branch or twig, and his smell.

"Good, now keep your eyes closed and find me."

"What the hell?! I want to rip your head off and you're acting like my teacher?!"

"Trust me, I'll piss you off again, but first I want to see how good your natural instincts are. They're heightened of course, but you have some of the best natural abilities I've ever seen besides mine."

I kept my eyes closed – not because he told me to, but because I could hear better that way. Closing off one of the senses forced the other senses to step up to the plate. I heard another crunch to the left…then the right. I turned to each of the sounds with my eyes closed. It didn't take long for Nikias to return to his normal asinine self again, as images started rushing through my mind. When the image stopped…oh, when that image or vision became clear, that was it! He would be in serious pain soon!

The image was *Mandy in the center of the arena. Her students and horses were circling her. She looked so sad. There wasn't the same vitality, the love of life, on her face. She was giving them direction on their lesson and asking them to do various moves, but with no enthusiasm. Suddenly she stopped and turned her attention to the hill leading to the house. Her students stopped circling and stared at their teacher. When the students looked up the hill I could then see where this vision was leading.*

I was standing at the railing of the arena smiling. Then Mandy spoke.

"Excuse me, can I help you?" Mandy was talking to me as if she had no clue who I was!

"That's right big brother! Your assumptions are correct. I have considered taking her memories of you and that little display is what you would be left with. She would just think you're some dork that's looking for riding lessons!"

I thought of nothing but ripping his head off but I felt numb. My body no longer belonged to me, but to a supernatural state of being; rage pulsed through every vein, every fiber of my being. I barely heard Damien yell in the background. It didn't matter; my mind no longer obeyed me, but the beast within.

Within seconds of changing, Nikias stepped out of the forest's edge and moved toward me.

"Told you I'd piss you off, Brother. By the way, that was a vision it will happen…soon."

"Stay away from her! I'm gonna rip out your heart and shove it down your throat!"

Suddenly, claws the size of my human forearm sprouted from my huge black paws. They dug into the ground as I lunged forward, with the intent and the need to kill my enemy. All my senses – hearing, vision, and smell – came to a full and vivid life and honed in on Nikias. Everything else around me was a blur, but my enemy was clear. I could see every black, shiny strand of his fur. He stood his ground as I closed the gap. His eyes were that crimson red; his head was low to the ground, and all four legs were spaced evenly apart to bring his body into a firm stance. He stood facing me head-on as I raced toward him, and I fully expected him to lunge at me. A thousand scenarios were running through my head, and that was probably my mistake. He knew I was off guard and not sure of his move. I kept moving toward him, and it only took seconds to reach…what…wait…what the…he had vanished.

I put on all four brakes, my claws automatically retracting. The heels of my paws took over and tore into the earth, making a trench beneath them. I tore up grass as I tried to stop. All this seemed to take forever, but I'm sure it was only milliseconds. I came to a complete stop and stood dumbfounded. I knew he wasn't invisible, at least not at the moment he disappeared. He stood before me one second, and the next his body was a blend of two different colors – black and gray – as if he were shot out of a cannon but faster than the speed of sound.

I knew he had sped off to the right, and I spun around in that direction the second I stopped. Not there. I took a deep breath and closed my eyes, tuning out every sound and smell except Nikias'. If he did run that fast, he would be out of breath and I'd be able to hear him.

Behind me, a crunching sound. I wheeled to face him but he was already in the air in full leap. I reared up on my hind legs to connect with his stomach and bring him down, but he twisted in mid-air just out of reach. My front legs came down with a heavy thud and I spun around to find my so-called brother about twenty feet from me. I lunged again with the same result, dirt and grass flying in the air as we played this game awhile longer. With each move and twist he made, I got better at anticipating them.

Something inside my head clicked and I focused on my adversary intently.

Nose to nose, we circled each other in the dirt, which used to be grass. Our eyes locked on each other, and every piece of fur on my body stood at attention.

"C'mon, chicken shit! You know how to take me down…DO IT!!"

I stopped circling and gathered every ounce of strength in my massive body. I saw his exposed throat. I twisted my head sideways and aimed for his jugular. Nikias bounced up, twisted over me and landed behind me. How does he do that?!

I spun around facing him again, and wasn't about to give him time to think. I lunged as fast and hard as I could, and this time he sprang up and backward into a back flip. But I had already anticipated this move and caught his back right foot in my mouth. I could taste the dirt from the pads on his paws and feel the fur from his foot on my tongue. I also tasted his blood. I yanked him from his leap and slammed him into the ground. Nikias actually yelped like a puppy. I kept picturing Mandy's face and became more enraged.

Growling sounds rumbled up from both our throats, but they didn't slow either of us. Nikias tried to pull his foot out of my mouth but did not succeed. I dug my teeth into the bones of his paw and he yelped again; but his vulnerability didn't last long. Nikias bent his body toward me and grabbed the back of my neck, flinging me over his head like a rag doll. He slammed me to the ground; but he didn't realize I would be able to keep the grip on his paw as I went sailing over his head and into the ground. His paw still in my mouth, Nikias was forced to flip over me, which frustrated him intensely. It was obvious that he had never come this close to being defeated.

I kept Mandy's image in my head so the rage would take over. Nikias' fury rose from him as he lunged at my neck a second time. This time I released the bloody paw from my mouth and took him by the neck. I knew I could not let go or he would overpower me.

I dug my teeth into the side of his neck and lashed at his side with my right front claws. Blood poured from the cuts I made, and he yelped louder.

"BOYS! Knock it off right this second!" A female voice bellowed at us. How I heard the voice over the battle I never figured out. I released the grip I had on Nikias and turned toward the voice. What? I was distracted and without the rage inside, my body phased back into my human form. I didn't even think about the absence of clothes. I could not take my eyes or mind off the image in front of me; even the young child who came running to our sides with clothes didn't draw my eyes away from the vision standing before us.

I quickly put the clothes on and then looked back at the place where the female voice had originated. For a split second I thought Damien had phased and he was so nervous that he sounded like a woman. That theory was quickly put to rest when I saw him still standing at the edge of the forest, also bewildered by the sight.

"Nikias, get to the house right now! You know better than to lose control, especially with your brother!"

"Mom, it's part of the training. I just got a little carried away. I wouldn't have let it go much further."

"Get home, NOW!"

"FINE! He's all yours! I'm outta here. Oh, Jesse – remember will happen very soon." I concentrated on the other Jaguar standing not twenty feet from us when Nikias broke out laughing from the edge of the forest. His cocky, smug laughter jolted me out of my trance and I realized what he had said.

"Nikias, I swear to God if you go anywhere near the girls I will kill you!" We had both phased back into human form, and Nikias was walking toward Damien when I yelled at him. He wheeled around to face me and his eyes were again red.

"You can't stop me, Brother. Besides, I'm bored and my work here is done. Have fun with the rest of your schooling. You'll love working with Mom." He laughed again, then turned back to Damien, who still stood motionless.

"Wait…what?! What do you mean, 'Mom'? Get back here!" I turned to look at the other jaguar, but it was gone. I looked at Damien and he shrugged his shoulders.

Nikias had already vanished into the forest. Damien ran into the clearing to my side.

"Look!"

I looked where he pointed, and there she was. She was a vision of beauty and looked to be about 25 years old. Ha! That's too young to be our mother, of course Nikias was toying with us. She stood in the clearing in a long, flowing white sundress, staring at us. Her complexion was a dark tan; she had dark brown eyes and long, straight black hair which hung down to the middle of her back, and flowed with the dress in the breeze. She was about five-three and very slender, not too thin but slender and toned.

She stood there, not taking her gaze off the two of us. Finally, Damien worked up the courage to break the silence.

"Who are you?" He stammered. There was a long pause before she answered.

"Think, Damien. Who do you think I am?"

"I have no idea. Stop playing games and just tell us who you are!"

"Honey, I am your mother. All three of you are my boys."

"Oh come on! Now this is ridiculous! First, Nikias is trying to convince us he's our triplet, which is a hoax. I think he's able to morph into any form he wants so he what, thinks we're so good-looking that he wants to be us? Now you're telling me that you're my dead mother?! You're about our age, which makes it even more ludicrous!" Damien and I waited for her response as she walked closer.

"My name is Trina, Damien. Trina Matthias, formerly Balcombe. I was married to your father, Petros Balcombe. I gave birth to triplets but was told that two had died. Of course, that was you, Jesse, and Nikias who had supposedly died. I was devastated but relieved that at least one of my boys had survived." She took a deep breath and looked at Damien, whose eyes were beginning to glisten with tears. I could tell he was trying not to believe her story. Trina looked back at me and continued:

"The first thing I want you to do is take off your right shoe and sock then look at the bottom of the foot."

"What?!"

"Just do it, please." Reluctantly we both did what she asked. Of course, it was easy for me as my shoes were in a shredded pile so I stood bare foot. I knew what I would find but didn't understand what that had to do with anything. I picked up my right bare foot and saw the birthmark, big deal.

"So, I have a birthmark. I knew that already."

"Jesse, look at Damien's foot and Damien you look at Jesse's." We looked at each others' foot and both of us nearly fell over. We had the exact same black, jaguar shaped birthmark in the same exact spot! I hadn't thought of that mark for years. Then this beautiful woman took off her right shoe and sock and lifted it for us to view. She also had the exact same birth mark!

"All of us have the mark which is how they know for sure you have the 'gene'. I'll explain more of that later. Jesse, if I'd had any idea you and Nikias were alive back then, I swear I would have found you and run away with all of you. Your father was violent, but I never dreamed how much more violent he would become after I got pregnant with you three.

Damien, when you were two he beat me so badly that I nearly died. I could hear you crying in your room, but I couldn't get to you. Every time I tried, Petros would throw me back down to the floor and kick me over and over. He threatened to kill you if I tried to get to you.

I must have finally blacked out from the pain and injuries, because the next thing I knew I was here, on this island! They told me I had been in a coma for two weeks and weren't sure if I would ever come out of it." She paused, trying to get a sense of how we felt about the whole new 'family' idea.

"You're right, Damien – if I were a mortal human it would be impossible for me to be your mother at this age. I was mortal when you were born and up until they brought me here. When I came out of the coma, I was told I went into a state of shock for another few days and they kept me sedated. After a few days had passed, I was well enough physically and mentally for the explanations, transformations and training to start." Trina – or whatever her name really is – looked back and forth between Damien and me. I truly did not know what to think at this point, but wanted to hear the rest of her story.

Damien, on the other hand, was furious.

"You expect me to believe this ridiculous story!? From what I know about our mother, she was a saint. She was kind and generous and never would have allowed our lives to be turned upside down like this! When dad was drunk, which was most of the time, I would run to a neighbor's house and hide. She told me all about my mom. But our psychopath father burned my mom to death when I was two! She's dead! Tell us who you really are!" Damien had taken three steps closer to the woman, and I could see the veins in his arms begin to bulge. I tried to calm him by placing my hand on his shoulder, but that only made him angrier.

"Knock it off Jesse! I'm fine! I just want the truth from this woman!" She stood her ground, even with Damien inching closer. She did not waver.

"Damien, I know this affects you the most. We were able to have two years together, even though you don't remember. We formed a very special bond in those two short years that can never be broken. It's hidden right now beneath your rage, but it is there. I didn't have that opportunity with Jesse and Nikias." She looked at me, tears streaming down her face. She was right; I had no emotional ties to our biological mother. Whether this story was true or made up, it did not affect me the way it did Damien.

"That's exactly why I want you to stop saying you are our mother! It's a lie!" Damien was beyond angry and went straight to "lava" mode. His phasing was much slower than mine or Nikias', but effective. His arms and neck began to pulse and his eyes turned the eerie red, which was usually followed by the beast.

This petite woman still stood her ground and did not look threatened or even frightened. She was only inches from Damien's face, yet she remained calm. He gradually phased into the Jaguar; this did cause her to step off to the side, but she still showed no sign of fear. I expected her to phase at any moment so she would be able to defend herself - but nothing happened. I decided I'd better get ready to defend her so Damien wouldn't have a murder on his conscience.

I stood watching them stare at each other. Damien's eyes fixed on the woman's eyes, his teeth bared and a low growl bubbled from deep within his belly and up through his throat. She still just stood there, but she must have sensed my anxiety.

"Jesse, it's okay. He won't hurt me."

"How do you know?"

"I wanted him to phase, as his instincts are more tuned in that form, and he will know – he will know it's really me."

"Yeah, well I'm ready and will take him down if I have to. Can he 'hear' us right now? He doesn't seem to notice that we're 'speaking' to each other."

"No, I have him blocked." She never moved or took her eyes off Damien during our 'conversation'.

Finally, Damien's body relaxed somewhat and he took two steps backward. I noticed one of the young boys from the village – or, cave-town, whatever it is – hiding behind a large boulder to our right. I figured he had clothes for Damien when he phased back into human form.

And slowly, Damien phased back. The young boy hurried to his side with shorts, tennis shoes and a t-shirt. Damien quickly put the clothes on, but his eyes never left the mysterious woman.

"Why didn't you turn or phase or whatever? I could've really hurt you. You weren't frightened at all?"

"You are my son, Damien. I knew you would feel the bond more intensely in the animal form than human. I wanted you to phase. I wanted you to know for certain that I'm telling you the truth." The woman never raised her voice, but maintained a calm, soft tone as she spoke.

"I'm not saying I believe you, but go ahead and finish the story and see if you can make me believe." Damien sat down on the grass, Indian-style, and the woman and I followed suit. We sat there in the middle of the clearing staring at each other. Well, okay – Damien and I stared at the woman and her eyes volleyed back and forth between Damien and me.

"Let's see, where was I? Oh yes, I remember." She cleared her throat and continued. "You see, our bloodlines go back to the sixteenth century and every child is raised preferably by the biological parents until they reach age 22 to 25. They are then brought here to start the 'change'.

My dad, your grandfather, has the bloodline, but my mother does not. If The Family feels they can trust the outside parent, then they will be brought into the very large circle later. It's very tricky, as you can imagine. Let me give you an example of how this all works…

Two people fall in love, one with the bloodline but not knowing, the other without. They marry at, we'll say age 20, and have a child. The mother, for example, and the child have the same bloodline. The husband obviously does not. The wife is abducted by The Family at age – oh, let's say age 22 – and is brought to the island. The wife spends months going through 'the change' then off to a school for the final teaching and training. The child is at home being raised by the child's father. He has no idea what has happened to his wife, which I think is cruel. But that's the way things are done.

Then one day, months later when the wife has finished her transformation and training, she is brought to a community in the United States that you will eventually be taken to, where she awaits her husband. Members of The Family abduct her husband and bring him to his wife. Of course, the child or children are also brought and taken care of by other members of The Family. The husband is reunited with his wife and told the whole sordid story. If the husband is able to handle being in this strange world, they will all be returned home, where they will continue raising the children. When the children reach the appropriate age, the cycle continues." Trina paused a moment to get a sense of our reactions. Both Damien and I were processing so she continued.

"It is difficult, when two people love each other and one will never age or die, and the other will do both. In some cases the non-bloodline spouse wants to be 'changed' as well, which is possible but difficult. It is extremely risky. When it is successful the spouse is immortal but has no abilities. They are able to remain with their loved one forever."

"Has anybody died from the 'change'?"

"Yes, Jesse. There have been cases where the process has gone wrong and that spouse has died. There have also been cases in which the outside spouse cannot handle the news or lifestyle. He or she is returned home safe and sound but their memory of the island and The Family is erased. He or she is taken home but without the spouse or children. They are led to believe their family has perished. Again, in my opinion, cruel but necessary. A story has to be told to the kids as well as they continue to live with their mother or father, whichever has the gene.

There have also been cases when the spouse who has the bloodline wants to return home with their significant other who can't handle the new lifestyle. That's a real challenge and has only happened twice that I know of. The Family had to erase the the non-bloodline spouse and children's memory and the spouse with the gene had to act as if nothing happened and all is normal."

Damien and I were still processing and didn't realize it was getting dark. Trina got up and held out her hands to each of us.

"I will tell you the rest of the story at the house. It's getting dark." I reached for her hand and Damien sat there, staring at her. I elbowed him in the side and he got up but did not take her hand.

"I don't know if I believe you, but I want to hear more. Let's go." We walked back to the house and the little round gentleman who had served our lunch had dinner waiting for us on the table, a new table not broken in half. They must have an endless supply of all kinds of stuff with Nikias living here. It looked like Nikias had already eaten, as there was a dirty, empty plate sitting on the table. We sat down and began eating, in silence.

After dinner, the three of us went into the living room where a roaring fire blazed in the fireplace. Three glasses of wine sat on the oak coffee table. We each found a comfortable seat on the leather L-shaped sofa in front of the fire. I couldn't help but wish that Mandy were here with me. It was a very romantic room – such a waste to be here with my brother and a woman claiming to be my mother. The mysterious woman continued…

"I was twenty-three years old when I was rescued and brought to the island. I was told by the chief that they hated my husband but couldn't interfere. They watched all four of us, mainly me, Damien and Nikias, as they were able to tell that you, Jesse, were with a good and loving family. They still kept an eye on you but concentrated more on the three of us. When your psychotic father became more out of control and decided on that dreadful day to do away with me, The Family stepped in just in time. Petros had beaten me so badly that day that I passed out, I guess for a long time as I was in a coma, as I told you before. His intention was, of course, to burn me alive. Oh, he was an evil man and I so regret every horrible second I spent with him, but I don't regret what he gave me – you three.

Anyway, I was told that he had a bonfire all prepared just outside our property. Petros carried my body to the fire and threw me on the ground. The Family told me that as he turned away for a split second, one of them sneaked up behind him and knocked him out. One of them planted an image in his head of me being thrown into the fire by his hands. That way, when he woke up he wouldn't know what happened but would think that he had passed out from being drunk, as usual, and killed me." She took a deep breath and tried desperately to hide her tears.

"When I got over the shock of learning I had nearly been murdered, I immediately thought of Damien. I cried and screamed at The Family members to rescue you and bring you to me. Several of them had to hold me down so they could explain the rest of our story and tell me why they couldn't get Damien yet. They said Damien's story would have to play out until he was of age or in a life-threatening situation. Since I was no longer in danger they were able to concentrate solely on you, Damien and Nikias.

Living with that maniac, Damien, you had come close to needing intervention many times, but you're strong and each time you found your own way. When my training and transformation were complete several months later, I was able to keep an 'eye' on you and Nikias. I would peek in on you, Jesse, from time to time, but your life was a paradise compared to the other two. I knew it was my fault that they had such a horrible life; I married that evil man."

"Why?! Why would you marry a man like that?! What in the hell did you see in that animal? I hated you for years! I hated you for being with him! I hated you for leaving us, and I hated you for leaving me with him!!" Damien was starting to get up, and I put my hand on his shoulder. His body was tense and his eyes were beginning to change color, but he finally relaxed enough to sit down again.

"Damien, you have every right to hate me. I don't blame you. When I first met Petros he was a different person. We had only been married for a year when things started going wrong – well, horribly wrong. Everything happened so fast. He lost his job, then

I found out I was pregnant. He had started drinking; the violence hadn't started, but he would raise his voice – it was building. I was afraid to tell him I was pregnant. When I finally found the courage he became enraged and started breaking everything in the house. It wasn't long before he took his rage out on me. When I was about four months along, I found out it was triplets. Petros wasn't with me when that news came to light. I kept that information to myself for as long as I could. As the months passed, he continued his drunken rages and would get angry about stupid things and turn the rage toward me. He beat me several times before you three were born, and thank God it was not fatal to any of you. Of course, I didn't find that out until much later. I was told the two of you had died.

When I was seven and a half months along, I had decided I'd better get it over with and tell him. I planned a special evening with candlelight and cooked his favorite foods. Petros had been out that day on more job interviews, and I was hoping he would have good news about a job. That would've made my news much easier to take. When he walked in the door I could tell that would not be the case, and he had been drinking. He usually would start drinking at home and then wind up at a bar all night. When he walked in already drunk, I knew the job hunting had not gone well, again.

It turned out that while he was in town a friend of his had congratulated him on the news about triplets. I couldn't believe it! I had only told one person and she had sworn not to say a word to anyone. So, he knew I kept that from him and the job interviews hadn't gone well. He was furious and told me he was going to beat me and the babies to death. Luckily, he was so drunk that he only managed to slap me across the face and then he fell backward. I was horrified and managed to get out of the house. I ran – well, hobbled would be more appropriate – to the road, and I guess someone was watching out for me, as one of our neighbors drove up and asked if I was okay. I told him no and asked him to please take me to the police station. For the first time, I was going to press charges on that bastard!

But, you three had other plans. On the way to the police station I went into labor!" She paused, and began twirling her hair between her fingers while staring into space. It was difficult to hear the truth, but even harder watching our mother relive the horror. Yes, I had come to believe that she was indeed our mother. I wasn't sure about Damien, but I believed her. I could feel every emotion she had swelling inside her right now. I could see the pain and anger she went through and still held onto after all these years.

She was seated between Damien and me. Without thinking, I scooted closer to her and took her hand. My touch brought her away from her dark memories and back to the present. One corner of her mouth turned up into a smile and she squeezed my hand, staring into my eyes. I could see the relief in her eyes that I believed her. She kept a firm grip on my hand as she continued the story...

"My neighbor, a nice young man, turned the car around in the direction of the hospital when he saw that I was in labor. I screamed at him, and I still feel badly about that to this day, to turn around and go to the police. I knew Petros would wake up soon and try to find me. The young man assured me that he would call the police as soon as we got to the hospital. I agreed and we continued on our way.

Once there, much of it is a blur. I remember that he helped me into the emergency area and waited by my side until they wheeled me away. I don't know what happened to him after that or if he called the police." Trina stopped again and stared at the fire.

"Come to think of it, I never saw him around the neighborhood after that day." I couldn't help myself and tuned into her thoughts. I couldn't make sense of them and the funny thing is, the old expression 'you can see the wheels turning' is not far from the truth. When someone has an epiphany, it does sort of look like wheels turning in their head.

"It all makes sense now. That neighbor must have been on Petros' and lawyer's payroll. I always wondered how Petros figured out so quickly that I was at the hospital. I wasn't due for another two months and if the neighbor had called the police like he promised, Petros would have gone to jail instead of showing his evil face at the hospital." She snapped out of it and looked at Damien and me. There must have been confusion on our faces as well, trying to figure out what in the world she was talking about.

"Sorry, now where was I? Oh yes – I found out from The Family that Petros had made an ugly deal with a scummy attorney to sell the babies. I'm sure Petros wanted all of you sold, but part of his plan was spoiled when I woke up too early and heard Damien crying at my side. The doctor was also on the payroll and convinced me that the babies and I were in danger and that I needed a C-section. He was my doctor so of course, I believed him. I was also two months early, so that made sense to me. I'm sure it was the plan of the doctor to wheel away all three of you before I woke up, and then tell me all three of you had died.

They did manage to get you and Nikias out of the room before I awoke and convinced me that two of you had died. I was devastated. Looking back on it, Damien, you might have been better off if I hadn't woken up early. Maybe you would have been lucky like Jesse and found a good home." Tears were beginning to glisten in her eyes, and they looked sad.

Both Damien and I were so engrossed in the story that we didn't notice Nikias standing in the doorway. "It's time to go. They're waiting for them."

"Okay, we'll be there in a minute." Trina glanced at Nikias and back to us.

"What's he talking about? Where are we going now?" Damien began to tense up again.

"It's time to get you two settled in at…well…" Trina looked down at her hands and chuckled. "School." Her eyes met ours, and I didn't have to look at Damien to know he was about to lose it.

"Excuse me? 'School'?! What in the hell are you talking about?" He began to rise from the couch but I grabbed his forearm and eased him back down. He sat, though barely, on the edge of the leather cushion.

"I tried my best to get The Family to let Nikias and I to do your training, but they wouldn't allow it. Immediate family members are not allowed to train. No exceptions. When I say exceptions, I tried to pull the 'royalty' card, but that's when they pulled the 'no exceptions'. I really thought we could keep you here but it's out of my hands. I will make you this promise though...in a couple of weeks when you're settled, I will come out and visit. We can continue this conversation then."

"You haven't answered my question! Where are we going?! And, wait, what...royalty?" Damien had stood, and this time I didn't try to calm him down. I wanted the answers as well.

"All I can tell you is that Buzzard will be your transportation again and you will be taken to a place far away. All will be explained, I promise. As soon as they allow, I will visit and continue telling you our personal story. Your family heritage will be explained at the school." What happened next was so quick that there was absolutely nothing I could do to stop it.

Trina's eyes turned crimson. As soon as I saw her eyes change, she grabbed me by the front of my shirt and flung me across the room. As I flew toward the doorway, my immediate instinct was to phase and attack. Luckily I was able to control it enough in that millisecond to realize that Trina had done that to get me out of harm's way. In the time that her hand released my shirt and before I landed, she had phased and was standing face-to-face with Damien. He was still completing his phase, though it was a little faster than the last time. The couch we had been comfortably sitting on and the coffee table were in different places. The couch was lying on its back facing the other direction, and the table was standing on end at the other side of the room. Trina must have sensed my tension or read my thoughts.

Jesse, it's okay. Stay where you are. Damien has every right to be furious with me

Don't speak like I'm not here! Of course I'm furious! I didn't ask for this. I didn't want this, and I didn't want the childhood – or should I say 'lack of childhood – I got. You and Nikias turn our lives upside down, drag us away from the loves of our lives, and expect us to lie down and accept this new so-called family. Jesse, did you forget that Nikias told us we'd never see the girls again?! Well, forget it! Damien took three steps closer to Trina, but she stood her ground again.

I promise you, Damien, that all will be revealed and make sense in the months to come. I don't know what Nikias was trying to do but you will see the girls again. If all goes well, you should be back with Cassie and Mandy by next Christmas. You can lead normal lives – well, as normal as possible – with normal jobs. You will basically be on call after training is over.

There was only about a foot and a half between Trina and Damien. I'm not sure which part of her comment got to him, but he leapt up and would have landed on her back had she not anticipated his action. She got out of his way and faced him on the other side of the room. They had switched places, but it took Damien a few seconds to realize this and he was facing the wall. He quickly turned to face her but before he could make his next move, Nikias got in on the action.

He appeared out of nowhere and stepped over me. As his foot cleared mine he phased and stepped between his brother and his mother.

Nikias, stay out of it! This is between me and her!

Whatever! If it was Jesse or anyone else, I would let you kill yourselves but this is our mother and I refuse to let you disrespect her this way. Come to think of it, I should get out of the way, cause Mom would kill you in less than a second.

Nikias, that's enough. Damien is right - this is between the two of us. He is not disrespecting me and has every right to be furious at me and the whole situation. And I don't know what you trying to do but don't ever lie to them again, you know they will see the girls again.

Whatever...fine, you two go ahead and kill each other. I don't care! Nikias phased back and left the room.

I looked at Damien and he had phased back. One of the 'helpers' was at his side with clothes.

Nikias peered back in. "Well, I don't care what your differences are, we have to go now. The Family is getting impatient." He turned and glared at me, then stormed from the room.

"Okay boys, let's go. I'll go as far as the meadow, then you'll be on your own for a while." Damien and I stood there watching Trina walk out of the room. We didn't read each other's thoughts, but we each knew what the other was thinking at that moment. Without saying a word, we walked out of the house and caught up to Trina and Nikias. Each time we went to the meadow we had to take the little speedboat out of the mountain and across the lake, and this time was no different.

When the boat stopped on the other side, Damien and I were the only ones to get out. Nikias wouldn't even look at us but Trina stood up and gave us each a hug.

"You boys take care of yourselves, and I will come and see you as soon as The Family gives me permission. Time will fly, you'll see. Then you can join your gorgeous ladies in the other world." I could tell Trina was trying to stay positive, but it was obvious that not being the one to train us and making us go wherever we were going was hurting her. Nikias just seemed irritated as usual. More than likely he was angry that he wasn't going to be able to beat the crap out of us during training. I'm sure he had been looking forward to that.

Hey Jesse. Don't worry, I'll take care of Mandy for you. Don't forget the image I showed you. That son of a bitch! I could feel my veins starting to swell and my body harden...when all of a sudden Damien and I were snatched up by Buzzard. Unbelievable!

Nikias, if you touch one hair on her head I will find you and kill you! As we flew higher I craned my neck and head as much as possible to keep Nikias in my sights. But it didn't last long, and soon he and Trina were out of our view. His thoughts still intruded…

Aw, Jesse…you have no idea what you're up against. By the time you're as strong as me, I'll have Mandy eating out of the palm of my hand — maybe literally. Oh, I forgot to tell you…I made both Cassie and Mandy forget you even exist! They have no memory of either of you or this whole experience! Then he laughed and turned his thoughts off. I couldn't get back in. What did he mean he 'made them forget'?

It hit me like a ton of bricks! Somehow he is able to erase someone's memories! Was this a joke? Was he just toying with me to piss me off? It worked. How do I…how do Damien and I get back to the girls? I could feel my skin getting hot and my pulse starting to race. What if I phase, right here and now? Would I be able to free Damien and I and get out of this creature's grip? I was snapped out of my thoughts. *Jesse, what's wrong?*

Nothing.

I know Nikias said something to you but he blocked me out again. Tell me what's going on with you two. I couldn't even read your thoughts! How is that possible? Did you figure out how he does that?

No. It's nothing, Damien. He's just being his jerky self and toying with me.

Chapter 5

The School

The more I struggled, the tighter Buzzard gripped me. It was useless. Buzzard had taken us straight up like a rocket, high above the clouds. There was no way to gauge which direction we were going or how far we had gone. For a creature the size of a mountain, he was very fast!

We finally began to descend into some white thick clouds, and the air was suddenly warmer. The further we descended, the warmer it became. All around us was white. As quickly as we had flown into the clouds we were out, and heading toward the ground at a very rapid rate. Buzzard was moving so quickly that I couldn't take in the surrounding area of our apparent landing stop. It looked as though he was going to fly through the ground, but about ten feet from the earth, he dropped us! Damien and I fell through the air. I tried to ease the landing by bracing myself with both feet and hands, but that didn't work out so well. I fell into my right side with my hand under my body. I felt and heard a snap. Damien crashed hard right next to me, and without thinking I jumped up to make sure he was okay. The excruciating pain in my wrist forced me back to the ground.

"Jesse, are you okay?" Damien reached over and tried to take my wrist, but I held it tight.

"I'm fine but I think my…" Suddenly my wrist snapped again and the pain was gone! It ached a little, but no pain. It had snapped back into place! I shook my head and turned to face Damien, who watched my 'healing' with awe.

"We really are freaks!" Damien managed to say.

"Yeah, I guess we are. Let's figure out where we are and if there's a way out of this hellhole." We seemed to be inside some sort of fortress. All around us was a brick wall, at least twelve feet high. We stood on a manicured lawn. At the far end – very far – appeared to be some sort of structure, but we couldn't tell what it was.

"Let's get over this wall and get out of here," I said. Damien nodded in agreement and we began running to the closest section of the wall. But the more we ran, the further away the wall was. Impossible. We started to run faster, but the wall moved faster and got further from our reach.

We stopped and tried to catch our breath. I turned a full circle and could see nothing but red brick for miles and miles. Except in one direction – that structure which we assumed was the 'school'. I didn't want to go toward it, didn't want to give in to this new life that was being forced on me. I only wanted Mandy and a normal life.

This time we didn't speak. We just started running toward another side of the wall. The same thing happened. The faster we ran, the further away the wall appeared. We tried twice more, then plopped down on the lush green grass to regroup. We had been sitting for only a couple of minutes when…

"Do you give up?" A female voice, but we couldn't see the body that went with it.

"Let us go!" I yelled, jumping to my feet and spinning around to find the source of the ridiculous question.

"Doesn't work that way. There is no way out until they let you out. But I'll leave you alone again if you want to keep trying. I have nothing else to do today."

"Show yourself, coward."

"Tsk, tsk. Is that any way to talk to a lady?"

"I don't care who you are, let us go!"

"You can leave when you have completed your training. Are you ready to begin, or would you like to keep trying to leave on your own? That only postpones the inevitable. But, be my guest. It's no skin off my nose."

Maybe we should just give up, Jesse.

NO! I want out of here now!

The voice continued. *Aw, that's too bad. Damien's got the right idea. Damien, come with me and you can get started. You'll be finished with your training and your brother will still be out here trying to climb the elusive wall.*

Get out of our heads!

"Okay, but you still need to come with me."

"Show yourself!"

"Agree to come with me."

"Are you kidding?" I was really getting frustrated by this point and realized I had clenched my fists so tight that my palms were bleeding. I opened my hands when I felt the pain, and instantly the cuts disappeared.

"What's the matter, Jesse? Your little hissy fit hurt your hands?"

"Fine! We'll go with you, but not until you come out of hiding." I had been looking toward the direction we had last heard the voice.

"Over here, boys." She had quietly moved behind us and when we turned, our jaws dropped. A beautiful, seemingly normal woman stood before us. Her eyes were a sparkling Caribbean blue. Jet black hair hung past her shoulders; she had dark skin and a smile that would knock any breathing man to his knees.

I finally managed to get control of my vocal cords. "Who... who are you?"

"I am Kyra. I will be your mentor during your first level of training. I know this is frustrating but believe me, the sooner you relax and go with it, the easier it will be. Same thing happened to me. I would have been a lot further in my training, but I fought it the whole first week, then kept fighting. When I finally came to my senses and realized how stupid I was being, three weeks had passed. Each level depends on your cooperation and how fast you learn your new abilities before you advance. What might take some a month may take another only two weeks. There are twenty levels of training.

Well, I've said way too much. Your advisor will explain the rest in orientation. I'm supposed to give you the tour and show you the ropes until you reach Level two. Are you ready to begin, or do you still want to try to conquer the wall?"

I looked at Damien and knew his answer.

"Fine, we'll go." Now I knew how prison inmates felt.

I'm taking you to your advisor, Adam, then I will show you around the entire school and to your room.

We walked through two gigantic iron doors that swung to the inside as we approached. I assumed this must be the main building. The floor was marble, dark gray with black swirls. The walls stood about forty feet high and massive chandeliers hung throughout the hallway lighting the way to the many rooms enclosed in this building. Straight ahead, about fifty yards away, was a wall of windows and doors. This building was very wide and long. I could barely make out one end or the other.

Kyra headed toward the wall of windows, but started up the stairs that were about halfway between the entrance and the windows. It was a U-shaped staircase and when we finally made it to the top, she stopped. Damien was behind her and hadn't reached the top step and nearly bumped into her. I stopped behind him and couldn't decide if I was irritated or scared.

Mr. Adam, are you ready for them?

Of course, Kyra. Bring them in.

She continued to the right; the hallway was very dark and kind of creepy. A door on the left squeaked open, very slowly. The three of us entered a room that looked like a library. Floor-to-ceiling built-in bookshelves covered three walls, stacked with books. The far wall was mainly windows, with French doors leading to a balcony. In front of the doors but facing the squeaking door, was a large mahogany desk. The advisor's back was to the French doors; I assumed he wanted to know who was entering his office. He sat in a high-backed leather chair, and on the top of his desk was a laptop, a plaque with his name, and a few pieces of paper. I didn't see any personal pictures anywhere in the office; no family, friends, pets... nothing. Sad.

"Hi boys. Welcome. I'm Adam and I'll be your advisor throughout this process. You can come to me any time with questions or concerns. I read your minds when you came in and no, there are no personal pictures in my office, Jesse. I keep my personal life separate from this life."

"I didn't mean anything by it, just curious." I have to keep reminding myself that everyone around me will have the same abilities I do, and probably more. I need to block my thoughts somehow.

"Kyra will take you around and then get you settled into your room. You will be sharing the room with two other students. Tomorrow morning I will meet you here after breakfast, and we'll discuss your schedules. Before you start your daily classes tomorrow you will go through orientation which will last all morning. A lot of questions will be answered during that time." He nodded at Kyra and we all left his office in silence. We passed another large office on the way down and Kyra explained that was the Dean's and we would probably meet him tomorrow.

We headed down the staircase and through the doors in the window-covered wall. It opened to a courtyard with what seemed to be hundreds of picnic tables. Surrounding the courtyard was a sidewalk in a box shape. The middle was all grass, tables and a small fountain in the center of it all.

"This is our outdoor 'take a deep breath' area. You can come out here any time you have free, but there is absolutely no horseplay, practicing phasing, fighting, etcetera. Think of it as an outdoor library. You have to be quiet. You can talk, but be mindful of the people around you who are trying to catch their breath. This training is physically and mentally exhausting and believe me, you will need this courtyard. We have an indoor mental break room as well, in case the weather is bad. Of course with our body temperature staying at 105 degrees all the time, weather isn't usually an issue unless you want to stay dry." She giggled then continued walking back toward the building.

"All the rooms in all these buildings are the dorm rooms. There are two levels to each of the three buildings, and each building has forty rooms. That's 120 rooms, each holding four students. Simple math tells us that we have 480 students at any given time. All of us are in the same training, just different levels." Kyra never slowed down as she spoke.

"Where are the classrooms." How ridiculous – going to elementary school at my age!

"The main building we just left holds all the classrooms, library, two gyms – male and female – the other quiet room, and the cafeteria. The administration offices are upstairs with the Dean and Advisor. I'm going to show you to your rooms to meet your roommates, if they're in, then we'll tour the main building." We had cut across the courtyard to the far left building and just as we entered one of the large archways of the first level...

Wow! How gorgeous are they?!

Hey, new students!

Kyra is so pretty!

Wish I could show those boys a thing or two!

Hey, Alastor, we could take them on!

Yeah, I know we could and it would be a fun massacre!

Why do they look so familiar?

I'm hungry.

Voices raced through my head. At first they didn't make sense. There were male and female talking a mile a minute and at the same time, making my head pound. I closed my eyes and stood there holding my head, trying to shut out the voices. Then it stopped. They just stopped as if I had pushed a button.

"Jesse, what's wrong?" Damien had noticed I wasn't behind him and walked away from Kyra to make sure I was okay.

"I don't know. It was quiet and peaceful, then all of a sudden I was hearing hundreds of voices in my head. It was like a bunch of different conversations all at once. Well, maybe not hundreds but a..."

I slowly turned to look at them and sure enough, they had all been staring and quickly turned away, pretending they didn't know what had just happened.

"Jesse! Jesse, what is it?"

"I can read minds again!" I turned to the curious crowd that was pretending we didn't exist.

Alright, since it's obvious you are all curious, I am Jesse and this is my brother, Damien. Don't pretend you don't notice us! One person answered...

Yeah, I know who you are. You guys are Nikias' brothers. My brother was here the same time he was. I'm Akylas.

I looked slowly around the courtyard to find him. Scanning the crowd, I noticed a young man sitting alone with his back to us. He was the only person who hadn't faced me. Everyone in the yard became dead quiet and stared at me. None of them would look at Akylas.

Why won't you look at me?
Is this better?

His table was at the far edge of the courtyard. I watched as he stood up and faced me. He was large – not fat, just big. He stood about six-four, with muscles the size of Godzilla. Obviously a body builder. Did he have a neck? I couldn't see it if he did.

We stared each other down for a couple minutes.

Yeah, that's better. I'm sure I'll see you around. I didn't want Damien to know I was 'speaking' to this guy until I could get more information.

Oh you'll see me around. Akylas gave me the once-over, then sat back down at his table.

I faced Damien, who was looking at me like I was from outer space. He was still blocked.

I said, "It's okay, let's go."

Kyra looked a little worried, but turned and resumed walking.

Our room wasn't huge, but bigger than a typical dorm room. It consisted of two oak bunk beds on the left and right sides of the room, with four small desks, two on each wall side by side. There was also an enormous walk-in closet with four small dressers, shelves for shoes and places on three walls to hang clothes. Names were taped to each of the drawers, including mine and Damien's. I opened one of my drawers and it was filled with socks and underwear. The other four drawers held t-shirts, shorts and jeans all packed inside. There were labels separating the batches of clothes which hung with each of our names. I hadn't even thought of that; we had been dropped here with nothing. Guess that's why – they provide everything. It's the least they could do for completely taking away my life!

"Let's go." Kyra seemed on edge and anxious.

"Is everything okay?" I asked. She was already at our door, seemingly ready to sprint out of there.

"Yeah, I'm hungry and it's almost dinnertime."

I knew she was lying but didn't press the issue. We walked back across the courtyard to the main building. Some students were sitting at the tables, but I didn't see Akylas. I noticed Kyra hesitated at his empty table, then continued walking briskly away. She showed us the line of classrooms along the hallway then stopped at some double doors at the end of the hall. She swung them open and we gazed into a gym that was at least four times the size of a high school gym. There were a couple of guys playing basketball, and they both stopped to check us out as we entered.

"This is the men's gym. All you guys have phasing practices here. The girls are at the other end of the other hall. As you can see, you can also play basketball when there are no classes here." She edged us out and closed the doors.

"This is one of the libraries." She opened a large – again, mahogany – door into a typical-looking library. There were several students studying. All eyes gazed at us, but not for long. They continued their studies as if the 'new guys' were no big deal.

Kyra closed that door and headed back to the main part of the building. We walked toward the stairs leading to administration, but went to the right of them to another narrow, short hallway. At the end of this hallway were two more large doors. She led us through the doors into the enormous cafeteria. There were a lot of big round tables with chairs positioned around them, maybe eight chairs to a table. It was buffet-style, starting at one end with plates and silverware, and continuing down two long walls in an L shape. We were the only students in the room, which I thought was odd.

"What time is dinner?" I had noticed a clock on the wall that said 5:56.

"Six p.m. sharp, breakfast is at 7:00 a.m. and lunch is at noon. If you walk in one minute late, you don't eat. They lock the doors until everyone is finished. You only have 20 minutes to get in, get your food and eat. First shift just left and we are the second shift eaters. There are three shifts so they boot us out quickly so third shift can get in here and eat."

No sooner had the words left her mouth than a floodgate opened! Waves of students came pouring through both sets of doors and immediately lined up to gather plates, silverware and food.

"You had better get in line. I'll see you tomorrow. Come here for breakfast, then head to Mr. Abram's office. He will give you your schedules. I'll catch up with you after lunch." She quickly got in line and we followed behind.

After getting our food we headed for an empty table. I put my tray down and looked around the room before sitting. I noticed everyone was staring so I decided to 'turn on' their thoughts...

Does he have a death wish?

I don't know but I hope there's some action.

Oh, grow up!

What's the big deal? I asked while looking around the room. I whipped my head around when I heard a familiar voice...

They're talking about me, this is my table and they're wondering if I'm going to beat the crap out of you for sitting here.

Akylas was standing at the chair next to me. Damien had seen him first and his face had turned pasty.

Kyra shimmied by our table taking her tray back up front. Wow, that girl eats fast. She gave her tray to the attendant, then snuck a glance at Akylas. Her glance turned to a glare as soon as he looked back at her. She spun her head around and sped out of the cafeteria.

So, are you?

What? Oh, beat the crap out of you? Nah, any brother of Nikias is a friend of mine.

Really? Why? He's a jerk!

Watch it. He did a lot for my family and my brother. Saved his life, actually.

You sure we're talking about the same guy??

Hey, I think Damien could use a glass of water or something. Should we clue him in or leave him in the dark?

"Damien, you still can't 'hear' us?" I asked.

"No, and it's driving me crazy! Stop talking like that and fill me in."

"Not much to fill in except Akylas claims our brother is a saint!"

"Huh? Nikias?"

"I didn't say a saint", Akylas chuckled. "He just helped my family. Hey, we better eat, time is wasting." We all sat in silence and ate quickly.

As if a bell had rung, everyone got up and took their trays to some large trash cans placed throughout the room, dumped the food, then gave their trays and utensils to the attendant at the far end of the room. Wow, exactly 19 minutes and everyone is done and heading out the double doors on the other side of the room!

I'll see you later. You guys are my roommates. The Family knew you were the only ones I would tolerate rooming with me. He didn't give me a chance to respond, just walked away.

I sat there a few more seconds, then realized Damien was giving me that look again.

"Okay, okay, let's go." We got up to join the line and returned our food trays.

We wandered around. then found ourselves in the outdoor courtyard. We sat on one of the cement benches.

"Jesse what do you think is going to happen to us? I mean if we ever get out of here? Will we see the girls again?" Damien was leaning forward with his head resting in the palm of his hands. Since arriving on the island and now here at this 'school', Damien seemed like a child that needed protection. I couldn't put my finger on it, but the vitality and brute strength I had witnessed during the kidnapping escape had vanished. I felt like he was my little brother that everyone was picking on and I had to protect him from all the bullies. And I would do just that, even though the only bully I could think of was Nikias. Hopefully we wouldn't have any trouble here.

"I don't know, D. I do know that we will do everything we can to hurry this process up so we can see the girls again. I promise you that." The sun was vanishing and we decided to find our rooms and turn in for the night.

Akylas was already there and lying on his bunk, the lower one on the right side of the room. Damien and I took the bunk on the left and I was relieved that they would not put a fourth person in here.

"Better get as much sleep as you can. They blow the horn at 5:30 am and you better be dressed and in the cafeteria by 6:00 am to eat. If you miss breakfast it makes for a very long day. You need all the strength and nutrition you can get." He rolled over and turned off his reading lamp that was attached to the bed above his head.

We took his advice and jumped in bed. I took the top bunk and lay there with my eyes closed. Images of Mandy crowded my brain. They kept changing, Mandy on horseback; Mandy on the beach; Mandy in bed smiling over at me; Mandy, Mandy, Mandy...

> *"Jesse! Where are you? Jesse!"*
> *"I'm here Mandy. I'm right in front of you! Why can't you see or hear me? Mandy!"*
> *Her body went limp and she fell to the floor. We were in her kitchen by the sink and I couldn't pick her up. I was on the floor with her trying to touch her but couldn't. My hands would go right through her. I sat there by her side and tears began to roll down my cheeks...*

A sound blasted me out of the dream. Horn?! Is he kidding? That was more like a bomb next to my ear!

"C'mon sleepy heads. Up and at it. Get dressed and meet me in the cafeteria." Akylas must have been up and dressed before that disgusting noise went off.

I jumped off the bed, almost kicking Damien in the head as he was also climbing out of bed.

"Oops, sorry about that. I'll have to get in the habit of looking down before jumping."

"It's alright, let's go." We got dressed and headed to the cafeteria again. Seemed like we had just left there. It was the same scene as last night. Everyone lining up like cattle waiting for their feed. It was one minute to six - when the clock struck six, the entire room came to life.

We got our food and joined Akylas at his table. I suppose it would be our table as well.

"Hey lazy bones. Finally decided to get your asses down to breakfast huh? So, I guess you head to the dean's office after this?"

"Yeah, Kyra told us he would give us our schedules and meet up after lunch. What's her story anyway? She was nice but got kind of nervous around dinner time."

"Yeah, she's a really nice person. She will teach ya the ropes. I don't know why she would have been nervous." I could tell he did know why but didn't want to share.

We finished our breakfast and found our way back to the dean's office.

"Hi boys. C'mon in." He had a very commanding voice. He shook both our hands firmly and sat us in front of his desk. He handed us each a piece of paper.

"Those are your schedules and on the back is a map with the areas you need to report to. Today will be an easy day, just getting you used to your new routine, teachers and classmates. Tomorrow will be the beginning of…hell." He had just as commanding a laugh.

"Your classes are not the traditional ones that you had in high school. You already know the basics. Your classes are divided into two parts, mental and physical training. Today in orientation you will learn the history of our families and The Family, we call them the elders even though they are our age. They were some of the first to be transformed and some of them will be here for your graduation. The next few weeks will be physically and mentally challenging. By the end of each day you will be exhausted, I guarantee it. There are 20 levels of training, each generally takes a week. Some may take longer depending on the person and that's fine. On average, each student is with us for five months.

Your first class starts at 8:00 am and each class is two hours, with four classes a day. You have two classes before lunch and two after. The rest of the day is yours, but you are to be in your rooms by 9:00 pm and lights out at 10:00 pm. This schedule is six days a week with Sunday off. Any questions so far?" We both shook our heads and he proceeded.

"Your advisor, whom you met briefly yesterday, is Adam and is next door to my office. He will be the one to counsel you if there is trouble or lag time in your training. He will work with your teachers and devise a plan to get you back on track. That doesn't happen often but it's nothing to be ashamed of if it does. Just concentrate and do what your instructors tell you and you should be fine. If you have other questions or concerns you may come to either of us." He stood up and walked around his desk toward us. Damien and I stood up and walked out the door.

"Go to the right and Adam is waiting. It was nice meeting you both finally and good luck." He closed his door and Damien and I stood there for a second. Without saying a word, we found Adam's door and walked in.

"Hi, nice to see you again. Have a seat." Adam was not as daunting as the Dean but I could tell he could hold his own if need be. He had dark brown eyes, almost black; about 6 ft. and medium build. I suppose for a guy he was ok looking. Come to think of it, everyone we encountered since arriving at the school was good looking and we all had dark complexions. I suppose we were all of Greek origin. Weird.

"I'm sure the Dean already told you the generalized routine of your schedules?" We both nodded so he continued.

"Well, let's take a look at your schedules and the map." We both put the paper in our laps and went over it with Adam.

"We decided to keep you both on the same schedule hoping that would help with the transition and maybe you could help each other out. Any questions?"

I said, "Actually, I do have one. Is it possible to get through the training before the five months is up?"

"It is but very rare and not recommended. At the end of each level is an exam that you must pass with a grade of 95% before moving on to the next. It takes the full week to get proficient in each. In the history of the school, which dates back to the 16th century, there have only been 12 students to excel and graduate early." His body language changed immediately. I could tell there was something he was not telling us. He got up and gestured toward the door.

"I'm going to take you to your orientation. Today will be the only day of this class and it is designed to fully introduce you to your new life, family ties, abilities and go over some of the class materials from each class. It will take you to lunch time then you will start your afternoon classes. Take a lot of notes during orientation as the information will come back throughout training and you will be tested on it. I have digital recorders that you can use while you're here if you're bad at taking notes. The recorders are to be turned in at graduation."

"We'll both take one, thank you." Damien looked at me as he said that and I nodded. Adam reached up on the bookshelf next to him and grabbed two small silver digital recorders. He handed them to us and directed us out of his office. We then followed him to the orientation room.

We shook his hand again and walked into the large classroom. I looked at the round black and white clock on the front wall, which read 7:45. We had fifteen minutes before orientation would begin. We found seats in the back of the room. I felt like I was in a high school science class. The room was set up with long high tables, two rows of about six on each side, with tall stools to sit on. There was a blackboard and teacher's desk at the front of the room. The difference between when I was in school and this was that instead of an old film projector there was a 50" flat screen tv attached to the wall above the blackboard. That was cool. There were 7 other students in orientation with us. Two female and the rest males, sitting silently. No one spoke, just sat there staring at the front of the room. Again, weird. I decided everyone was as nervous and apprehensive as Damien and I.

The long silence was broken when a beautiful woman walked in. As usual, she was early to mid-twenties; tan complexion; long straight black hair, but her eyes reminded me of Mandy's.

"Good morning class. My name is Leda. I am your orientation instructor as well as your mental instructor. I will be the one teaching you the fundamentals and fine tuning mind reading and communicating with your mind. The other mental class will include visions, planting visions and dreams. That will be taught by another instructor. Those classes are always in the afternoon after lunch and your physical classes will be in the morning after breakfast." She looked around the room at the nervous students.

"Before we begin let's go around the room and introduce ourselves. Tell me something about yourself and how you feel about this process so far. Don't be shy." She had a beautiful smile and tantalizing voice. She looked to her left at one of the girls sitting in the front.

As Ms. Leda went around the room she wrote the names on the board, including hers. When everyone was done, the names on the board were Alexa and Chara for the two girls, then mine and Damien's. The other males were Adrian, Galen, Colyn, Darius, and Demitri.

"Okay let's get started. Chara, would you pass these to each student?" She held out nine binders that were about an inch and a half thick. The binders were sectioned into four parts: The Beginning (the 16th Century); Legends and Facts; Royalty Members and Our Purpose.

"We'll go over everything in the binder and then take a fifteen minute break. The rest of the time will be videos. Easy morning for the first one. Before we begin, I want everyone to take off their right sock and shoe and look at the bottom of your foot."

Well, Damien and I knew where this was going but the rest of the class looked confused. We had our shoes and socks off and our feet resting on our left leg before any of the others had started with the exercise. When everyone was in the same position as Damien and I she instructed us to look at our neighbor's feet. Ms. Leda had also taken her shoe and sock off and was sitting on the edge of the desk.

She continued, "Every one of us has the same birthmark in the same exact spot. Cool huh? This is how they determine if we have the gene and to this day, no one knows how the birthmark started. With each and every one of us, the Collector had to find a way to see that mark before taking us. I'm not sure if you've heard that term yet - Collector. The Family assigns a Collector for each new student. Whoever grabbed you and brought you to the island, our starting point, was your Collector. All of you met Buzzard. He collects all of us with your Collector."

"How long have you been here?" Chara asked the instructor.

"My transformation happened almost twenty years ago. After my training they offered me a teaching position since that was my profession in the other world. I had no family left and no kids or significant other. It was a no brainer for me to take the job. I love it here.

Okay, let's get started. Open your binder to the first tab labeled, The Beginning." Leda walked up and down between the rows of desks while we found our page. She went over that section and patiently answered questions, mainly from the girls.

Our whole situation, family ties, abilities...all so surreal! The information she gave us was interesting but sounded like the start of a science fiction book.

After orientation we gathered our binders and all headed to the cafeteria for lunch. On the way, the others were chattering about what we had learned.

Damien still couldn't communicate with his mind so he spoke out loud.

"The Family and elders must think they're God! Who are they to decide how we will live our lives? What if we don't want to be part of their army against evil? Give me break!" He was still very agitated and resentful about being here. I felt the exact same way but I have always been able to bottle up my emotions. Sometimes it would feel like a tornado, hurricane and erupting volcano inside all at once but I would usually go to the boxing gym in my town and punch some bags.

Chapter 6

Training Begins

After lunch we found our way to one of the training fields. On our map it showed 4 training fields with each of the instructors' names at the top. Our class scheduled showed the name Alastor, field #3. The fields were side by side separated with grass paint like you would see at a football or baseball game. Each the size of a football field and numbered at the top. Ours of course, had a big white "3". We spent the next two hours in grueling physical training. By the end of the day our legs felt weak, even though Damien and I were both in good physical shape.

The days and weeks seemed to fly by, filled with hours of strenuous physical training followed by more hours of honing our mental and other "skills". By the end of each day, we were too exhausted to think of much besides just falling into bed. Damien and I had gradually been forced to believe that everything Trina had told us was the truth.

Four Months Later

One day in the middle of field training, I got a feeling that shot through me like a bullet. I clutched the sides of my head and fell to my knees.

"Jesse, what's wrong?!" Damien was standing next to me waiting for the instructor to make his next move.

"Shhh...I see him...he's in a field and he's...uh, he's watching... NO! It's Mandy!"

"What are you talking about? C'mon we gotta go!" I felt his hands trying to coax me to a standing position, but then I lost the sense of everything around me and caught a glimpse of Nikias. I had to quiet my thoughts and 'find' him.

I found Nikias sitting in a field – or was it a pasture? Was he on part of the island we hadn't seen? I got behind him to see what he was looking at. Oh my God! That's Mandy's house! What in the hell is he doing? Wait, I haven't been able to check on her for all these months. I haven't 'seen' her since before she made the deal with the devil to give up the search and go home. I stood behind Nikias for a few more minutes to see if I could figure out his mischief. I had to really concentrate so I could stay here and block him. He couldn't find out I was 'here'. Neither one of us were 'here' physically so it took more strength and concentration to stay and keep Nikias from sensing my presence.

No sooner had I knelt down behind him in the field, suddenly we were in Mandy's bedroom! A vision of beauty I hadn't been able to see in so many months – ever since Nikias had 'blocked' my view. My mind and body melted. Nikias snapped me out of it when he mumbled to himself in his mind...

"That's it, Mandy. Sleep...I'm going to have some fun now and see if your memories will stay in your dreams. I haven't had time to check on you for awhile. I need to make sure my little – hmm, what do I call it – loss of memory worked. The last time I snuck into your dreams and pretended I was Jesse standing on the hill worked like a charm. You thought it was him in your dream, but you woke up and didn't remember Jesse at all. Keep sleeping your peaceful dream, and in a minute it will get darker. But I need to check the rest of the house and make sure Sam is sleeping." He laughed his obnoxious 'I'm up to no good' laugh. I hated that laugh.

I let him leave to check on Sam...wait, who? It didn't matter at this point. I didn't say anything out loud or in my head and concentrated on getting into Mandy's head first. It occurred to me that Nikias must have put all his walls down with Damien and me as he didn't even notice my presence. Or maybe I'm getting stronger with the training the last three months. Wait...he said memory loss and he pretended to be me in a different dream?! He did it?! He took her memory?! But she kept her end of the bargain! She stopped looking for us! That bastard!

I had to keep my cool or he would 'hear' me. But when I see the son of a bitch in person, I will kill him!

I watched her closed eyelids move as her eyes rolled. Her deep sleep must have begun and I knew it was now or never. I concentrated and closed my eyes. I felt myself floating, then black silence for a moment. I did it; I was in her head...her dreams. We were standing in her kitchen, she was looking out the window and I was a few feet behind her. I whispered to her hoping Nikias would not 'hear' me and jump into her dream.

"Mandy, it's Jesse. Turn around and please don't be afraid. I just figured out what he did to you. I'm so sorry! I'm so sorry you and Cassie had to have any of this madness invade your lives. You don't deserve any of this. But I have to get through to you before he figures out I'm here. Think, Mandy. Remember me, remember us. Please. He couldn't have taken all of us from your memory! It has to be there somewhere! The love we felt so quickly. Nobody could take actual feelings, could they? Mandy, please try to remember." *I spoke to her but she didn't move. She just stared out the window overlooking the barn and arenas. I walked closer, reaching my right hand out toward her shoulder. As I was about to touch her, I was yanked back to the field, out of her dream!*

"Jesse, give it up! Her memory of you is gone and will never come back! How the hell did you get here anyway, little brother? For that matter, how did you find me or my 'essence' here at the ranch? You're not supposed to be able to 'reach' out to anyone outside of school until *graduation. Your training must be going well. I'm impressed. I didn't even excel that quickly. Well, I'll deal with that later. For now I'll have fun listening to you beg her to remember. "Aww Mandy, please remember me, it's Jesse!" He tried to imitate me but he wasn't even close. What a son of a bitch!*

"Oh such tough language coming from a saint like my little brother! I would say all three of us are sons of a bitch but I sort of like Mom so I won't speak badly about her." Nikias then took us back to Mandy's dream. She still stood motionless at the window. Nikias leaned in toward her right ear and whispered...

"Mandy, wake up and forget this dream. We'll try again later when there isn't an audience."

"NO! Leave her alone! Mandy, it's Jesse! Don't wake up yet! Don't listen to him! Remember us, you and me! You nicknamed me Scooby and I nicknamed you Skittles. Think! I know you can remember." I ran across the room and stood in front of her, staring at her, right into her soul. But she didn't see me. She stood there like a statue. I reached up to touch her hair but...

I felt myself being thrown across the room — which is weird, since we were in a dream, but it felt very real. I hit a wall and came down staring again at Mandy. She had snapped out of it somehow and the fear in her eyes made my heart ache. Nikias went invisible to her, but very real to me.

"Never mind, Mandy it's okay to wake up. I'll try again later. Wake up! I don't want you to see any more of this. Wake up!"

"OH No, Mandy, you need to see him get his ass kicked!"

"Mandy, WAKE UP! I love you and I'll see you soon!"

I was yanked out of the whole situation somehow, but not before I saw her open her eyes! Thank goodness, at least she's safe for a little while. I stood up straight and Damien grabbed my arms to steady me. I was dizzy and sweating profusely.

"Damien, I have to get out of here! Mandy's in trouble!"

"I know. I saw the whole thing. I'm not sure how, but somehow you sucked me in without knowing. Or maybe I'm so sick of being in the dark that I followed you. Either way I feel free, finally! And you're right, WE have to get out of here because both the girls are probably in danger."

"This is crazy. I've been able to do all of our abilities except check on Mandy, until today! You have been able to do everything but read minds and enter dreams right? But today you were able to do both? He is losing his hold on us! The timing couldn't be more perfect." I grabbed Damien's arm and started running.

"Where are we going?" Damien asked, running beside me.

"Finding a way out of here!"

We started running and Alastor, our field training instructor, yelled at us.

"Get back here!"

"Damien, phase NOW!"

Damien was still a little slow at phasing but mine for some reason, had always been instantaneous. He finally completed and we continued to run in our jaguar form. We hadn't gotten far when another jaguar appeared in front of us. All eight of our claws dug into the earth to slow us down, then finally to a stop. The three of us stared at each other for a few seconds. I thought it was Alastor but quickly learned it wasn't.

"Boys I told you I would visit as soon as I could. Looks like I showed up just in the nick of time. Where do you think you're going?"

"Trina, this is none of your business! Get out of our way!" I wasn't about to let our mother stop us.

"You three will always be my business. You need to go back. You're not finished with your training and we need you in tip top form."

"Why?" Damien asked.

"I can't explain yet but you have to trust me."

"No, that's not good enough! The girls are in danger with Nikias and I will not stay here while he plays around in Mandy's head!"

"Jesse, Mandy is fine. Nikias and I have been working together but I lost track of him for a brief time. I caught up to him when you had entered Mandy's dream just a few moments ago. I got you safely out of

there and then handled your brother. Let's just say, when he confessed his activities with Mandy, her family and friends, I made him undo everything. He won't be bothering any of them again. You both must believe me, the girls are fine. A bit confused but fine."

"Wait, what do you mean 'her family and friends'?"

"He admitted that by taking Mandy's memories and planting new ones, he had to do that to everyone around her. But everyone is fine and back to normal."

"Yeah right! I'll bet he's already gone back and turned their lives upside down again! He's a menace and I don't understand how you can trust him!"

"He is…well, mischievous and impulsive. He doesn't think before he acts and that can be dangerous, but he is family and has good instincts. His abilities are very keen and strong, like yours Jesse. You haven't even tapped into all you can do yet. I know you hate hearing this but you and Nikias are very much alike, not just in looks, but in instincts and abilities. In fact, I think you are stronger than your brother and that infuriates him."

"Then that is all the more reason for me to return to Mandy and keep her safe."

"He won't cross me, honey. I told him to leave all of them alone and he will. I'm sure that doesn't make you feel better but you're going to have to trust me. I promise to keep an eye on all of them but you have got to finish your training. Time is running out!"

"For what? What is going on?" Damien was getting impatient and I was beyond infuriated.

"Please, just trust me and get back to your training."

We all phased back into our human forms and the ever-present little helper ran up with clothes for all of us.

Buzzard suddenly appeared from the sky and picked up Trina climbed aboard.

"I love you boys – please, just do what your instructors say. It will be over before you know it and all will be explained!" She then disappeared into the sky.

"Fine! Let's get back to class." Damien and I walked through the field and as we got closer I could see Alastor's eyes turning crimson.

"Sorry about that sir. We don't have much of an excuse except to say that I thought a loved one was in grave danger."

"If you ever do that again you will be expelled! There have only been two students expelled in our history and believe me, it isn't pretty. We obviously cannot let you return to the 'real' world until you are done with training."

"Okay, okay...it won't happen again!"

We finished our classes for the day and headed to the courtyard. As we walked up the hill toward the massive school, I could not shake the feeling that there was extreme danger around the corner.

"Hey, isn't that Akylas and Kyra over there?"

"Yeah it is, let's go see if they know what's going on."

Kyra and Akylas were sitting at one of the tables in the courtyard and seemed to be having a quiet conversation. We decided to interrupt.

"Hey guys, can we join you?"

"Sure, have a seat." As we sat down I noticed all eyes on us but could not 'hear' anyone's thoughts. Really? They are blocking us?!

"Akylas, do you know what's going on? Our mom paid us an unexpected visit today in the field and said time was running out. What the hell is going on?"

"That's what we were just talking about. We heard about your little escape plan and almost getting expelled. What were you two thinking?! You know you can't leave until They say you can."

I explained, "My brother was messing with my head and I thought Mandy was in trouble." They both looked at Damien. I started laughing.

"No! Not Damien, Nikias."

"Oh okay." We all started laughing until we saw three of our instructors walking quickly into the building.

"I seriously want to know what's going on!" Damien whispered.

"Block your thoughts to everyone but Kyra and me."

"What? Why?" Damien asked while moving his head closer to us.

"Just do it." Damien and I were confused but complied.

"Kyra is a mentor as you know, and has access to the Dean's office more than the rest of us. Kyra, you tell them what you overheard."

"Well, I went upstairs two days ago to talk Abraam, you know, the Dean. I got to the top of the stairs and heard voices coming from his office. I couldn't tell who they were but I'm sure it was most of the school staff and others. They were almost whispering so I figured it had to be important. I couldn't make out what they were saying -they have obviously blocked out anyone but themselves to keep us in the dark- so I moved closer. I caught some of the conversations, enough to know that some Family members have betrayed them. I don't think they know who went rogue but whoever they are, they are helping someone or more than one, murder those with our genes before they are transformed!

I don't know if you've noticed the last few weeks that the staff around here has been on edge and acting weird. I think they are getting us all ready for a war but they don't know who the war is with." Kyra took a deep breath then looked down at the table. Akylas reached over and took her hand. They both squeezed each other's hand and stared at the table.

"How do they know who to go after? Only The Family knows who has the genes right?" I couldn't stand it, I knew something bad was around the corner.

"I think whoever betrayed them, got the list of people with the genes and my guess, it was an inside job. I just can't figure out why. Why kill any of us? We're not bad and don't hurt anyone. If anything, we protect people or are being trained to help protect. It doesn't make sense."

Akylas interrupted. *"Let's go eat and forget about it for now."* I knew he was right but I couldn't forget about it. Even though Mandy and Cassie didn't have the gene they were in the middle of this because of Damien and me. I decided after dinner I would try to 'talk' to Trina. She had to know more.

When we finished we headed back to our dorm and the four of us tried to put our heads together but came up with nothing. I told them I would try to contact Trina but the more I tried the more frustrated I became.

"Dammit! She must be blocking us."

"Well, let's turn in and try again tomorrow." Akylas and Kyra left while Damien and I sat there dumbfounded.

"Okay Jesse. Let's go to bed. We'll try again tomorrow like Akylas said."

"Alright, good night."

"Good night."

I lay in bed wide awake, thinking and getting angrier by the minute. I couldn't decide who I was most angry at - Nikias for his stunt with Mandy or at the phantoms who were hurting and killing innocent people. Probably both. I finally closed my eyes and decided to concentrate on Mandy. She needed to know everything would be okay and I needed to find out for myself if Nikias really did undo everything, bastard...

"Mandy, can you hear me?" I waited and concentrated on her house. I needed to 'find' her. I found myself in her kitchen but she was nowhere to be found. I knew she wouldn't be able to see me but I really wanted her to 'hear' me. I then heard a noise from the other room. A television? I walked past the dining room into the living room and someone was sitting in the recliner watching tv. I was behind her and sure it was Mandy. It looked like she had lighter hair though, really light. She must have dyed it.

I stood there motionless until I couldn't stand it any longer.

"Mandy, can you hear me?" I knew no one else would be able to hear me since I kept Mandy's face embedded in my brain and spoke to only her. I figured no one else would be there unless her barn manager or secretary made themselves at home in her living room.

She didn't turn around. She really can't 'hear' me? I must be losing my touch or something. Wait, she's getting up. I have to make her hear me!

"Mandy, you have to hear me!" *She turned around and headed toward me but... it wasn't Mandy. I had never seen this girl before. She was a teenager! What the heck...oh, wait, one of her students maybe? The girl walked right through me and headed toward the kitchen.*

"Mandy, I'm gonna make a sandwich, you want one?"

"Sure, thanks Sam."

Sam? That's the name Nikias mentioned a few months ago! She must be one of her students. At least I know where Mandy is now. I heard her call from upstairs. I took a step toward the stairs when I heard a disturbing newscast from the TV. I turned back around to watch and listen. It started with the music that news stations have when they are interrupting a show for breaking news, and a newswoman came on from an amusement park...

> "This is Sara Jackson live from KNS News. We're sorry for interrupting your program but we are at the scene of another horrific death. I'm standing close to the roller coaster at Six Flags in Atlanta, Georgia. If you have not been following this terrible story I will give you a brief recap. I want to warn you that details and images may be too graphic for young viewers.
>
> Several months ago in the desert of Nevada officials discovered what they now believe to be the first victim of the most bizarre and violent crime in history! The victims simply implode! Each body has been found in the middle of a field, in an empty parking lot or an abandoned building. Their entire bodies explode from the inside out! When the autopsy was conducted on the first victim, it was thought he had been blown up somehow. As they got further into the autopsy, this victim had actually imploded – he blew up from the inside out. It took weeks

to identify him but before they did, three more victims turned up in Nevada. And it didn't stop there…

There have been eighty-one victims so far, including today. The locations range from Nevada, California, Texas, Arizona, Colorado, Washington state, Montana, Nebraska, Iowa, Illinois and now Georgia.

There is no apparent pattern. The victims range in age from 13 to 20; hair color varies; victims are both male and female; tall, medium, short stature; thin, heavy; no traceable pattern has been found yet except they are young.

This terrifying and grisly series of killings has had officials stumped for months. There are no clues and no motives. None of these victims have any connection to each other. No one seems to know how a body can implode without the help of a device such as a bomb implanted inside. No devices or even traces of explosives have been found in any of the victims.

What makes this particular victim stand out from the rest is that it happened in front of hundreds of people. As I said before, all the bodies so far have been found in remote or deserted areas. Is the killer, or killers getting careless? Maybe he or she is getting bored and wants to step up the challenge?

The victim has not been identified yet pending an autopsy and notification of the family members."

The reporter walked over to a crowd of people holding each other and crying. It looked like they had locked down the park. Just as the reporter was about to interview witnesses Sam came back into the room with her sandwich and changed the channel.

This news must be what Kyra heard about. I stood there for a moment trying to process the news report. When Mandy walked into the kitchen behind me I was snapped out of my trance. I turned to look into those beautiful auburn eyes. I wanted to grab her, hug her so tight and never let go. I was about to 'speak' to her when Sam interrupted *my thought process again and Mandy had walked right through me toward Sam.*

"Mandy, can we rent a movie tonight?"

"Sure. What do you want to watch?"

"I don't care except nothing scary."

"You take all the fun out of movies." Mandy laughed then turned around toward the kitchen. I waited for her to walk through me again but she stood there staring right at me! Could she see me? Is that possible? Before I could figure it out I was snapped back to reality.

"Dammit Jesse! You are more stubborn than Nikias! I told you Mandy and everyone around her are fine and you need to concentrate on training!" Trina was the one who brought me back and I was furious!

"Why did you do that?! I was about to 'talk' to her. I wouldn't have stayed long and we are done training for the day! What is your problem?! Could it have to do with the murders going on back in the states? You better tell me what you know or I will keep going back. I'm a cop, remember? I won't stop until I know the people I love are safe." We were in our dorm room and our yelling of course woke up Damien and Akylas.

"Fine. You three, come with me." We walked through the adjoining building to the cafeteria.

"Stay here, I'll be right back." Trina walked out leaving the three of us dumbfounded and alone in the empty cafeteria.

"Jesse, what the hell is going on and why is Trina back so soon?" Damien finally broke the silence.

"I sort of went to Mandy's and Trina must have been there watching out for her. I don't know but she snatched me back just as I was about to reach out to Mandy. Before Mandy came downstairs there was a news report on TV. There have been 81 murders in the last few months with people imploding! Who do we know that can implode a human being?" Both Damien and Akylas stared at me waiting for the next words to come out of my mouth.

"Wait a minute. How were you at Mandy's watching the news?" Damien was completely missing the point.

"I went back to see for myself that she was safe and the television was on. This reporter, Sara Jackson, recapped the last few months. The latest victim was found today at Six Flags in Georgia. Ms. Jackson said that made 81 victims and they have no clues or motives." Trina returned with Mr. Abraam.

"It's obvious that none of you are going to concentrate on training until we fill you in." Mr. Abraams said with much irritation in his voice.

"This must not go any further, no one can know what's going on until we say. Do you all understand? Absolutely NO ONE!"

"Yes sir." Damien acknowledged then looked at Trina. "I thought you left today."

"I did but came back about an hour ago. I will be back and forth the next couple of weeks until your class is ready. Now, listen to Mr. Abraams and pay close attention." I felt like I was back at the Academy having no control over my life.

"We - The Family - were alerted to the situation a couple of months ago and have been following and investigating. We have moles throughout the world trying to find the person or persons behind these killings. We still don't know much except some of our own have betrayed us and are "hiding" the real brains behind the killings. We discovered some files on the computer had been copied. They were names and addresses of all the people with the gene. We know who the traitors are, as only so many of us have the password to those files. Unfortunately, we can't find them. We can't figure out how they are hiding themselves or where. We also know that others have somehow been recruited and probably brainwashed into being, for lack of a better term, their soldiers.

Our theory is that the mastermind or minds behind this somehow convinced the traitors to help him/her or them into getting the locations of the people with the genes. They obviously are trying to kill off the young people who have the gene before they reach the age of transforming. As you know, once the transformation begins, we cannot be killed. It must be someone with a deep grudge against us, but we have no idea why or who." Mr. Abraams took a deep breath then directed his attention to Akylas and me.

"You two have shown the greatest instincts and ease of all your abilities in the history of our Family. Akylas, we have not seen such strength; and Jesse, we have never seen someone slide into our abilities the way you have. Both of you have well exceeded any of the students from day one. Because of that, we need you to be in prime shape as The Family is heading into the worst war that we have seen in over 100 years." He looked at Trina to continue.

"Damien, you're very intelligent and you're computer savvy. We desperately need your skills. We want the five of you, when the time is right, to lead this war. Track this maniac down and get him or them before they kill more of our innocent young people.

We have no idea, as Mr. Abraams mentioned, how many of us have betrayed us. We don't know what you'll be walking into. In the next two weeks while you finish your training, we will be diligently trying to find the person or persons who are ultimately responsible. We need to find the masterminds and eliminate them. That will chop off the head of the snake and their soldiers will have no choice but to surrender. We are hoping this whole thing will be over by the time you finish training but if we fail in locating the devil then it falls to the five of you."

"What five are you speaking of? Don't think for a second that I didn't catch that one. I could tell by the look on her face that she didn't want to tell me but I could care less.

"You, Damien, Akylas, Kyra…" She paused and took a deep breath and in that instant I knew who the fifth person was. Nikias!

"Yes Jesse, Nikias. You two are going to have to put your differences aside until this is over. Innocent people are dying. They are killing our future!" I couldn't argue with that but the blood in my veins ran hot as I heard his name.

Mr. Abraams spoke up then. "Okay, go to bed. Jesse and Damien, stay away from Mandy and Cassie. Your mother is watching out for them. Also, don't say anything to Kyra yet. We will handle telling her." He said as he ushered us out the door.

We walked silently to our dorm room and crawled into our beds. All of us blocked each other out of our thoughts so we could have privacy.

The next morning began as usual. The horn blowing; all of us jumping out of bed; getting dressed and heading to the cafeteria like a herd of cattle. All the students were babbling like a bunch of high school students gossiping about the people they didn't like. The three of us had to keep everyone blocked out of our thoughts to keep the news we had learned a secret.

When classes were done for the day the three of us gathered in the courtyard. We wanted to quietly discuss strategy but just as we were about to begin, Kyra walked over to the table.

"Hey guys. I have been looking for you all day. What's going on? Don't tell me it's nothing because I tried reading any of your thoughts walking over here and you're all blocking me! Spill the beans, dudes." She sat down next to Akylas and we could tell he would crack under her pressure. It was obvious he was a goner, head over heels in love with this beauty.

Damien and I stared at him, still blocking Kyra.

Akylas, don't do it. I had to get my two cents in before he opened his mouth.

Kyra snickered, "Akylas, come on. You know you want to tell me and you know I'll get it out of you eventually so you might as well come clean." She took his hand and stared into his eyes.

"I can't Kyra. I'm sorry but I promise I will fill you in as soon as I can." He squeezed her hand, hoping that would calm her down but it made her angrier. She threw his hand back at him and stood up.

"Fine! Come on, we have to get ready for our graduation. In case you forgot, we get out of here in two days!" They had been here one month longer than us and were scheduled for graduation. I had forgotten about that and wondered how that would affect the 'mission'. Damien and I weren't supposed to graduate for another month, yet Mr. Abraams and Trina had mentioned two weeks. Akylas gave us the 'sorry guys but gotta go' look and walked away with Kyra.

"We're supposed to do this together. How will that work Jesse? They leave a month before us."

"Trina and Abraams said two weeks last night but I'm not sure what they're going to do with Akylas and Kyra in the meantime." I decided Trina must be close and I would ask. I tried contacting her through the elusive brainwaves but she didn't respond.

"I don't know Damien. Let's go find dear ol' Mom or Abraams and find out." We walked to the administration building and headed up the stairs to his office. We turned the corner in the hallway but I stopped cold, and Damien ran into the back of me.

"Jesse, what's the matter with you? Warn me the next..."

"Shhh..." I heard voices coming from Abraams' office and I recognized two of them. It was Nikias and Trina.

I whispered to Damien to block anyone from his thoughts so they would not know we were near.

"What?! You still don't know who this asshole is?!" Nikias was obviously aggravated.

"Nikias, keep your voice down and watch your language." Trina scolded him. "We are doing everything we can, but our hands are tied - which is why we need to accelerate your brothers' training and get all of you in the field full time. Akylas and Kyra are graduating but we will keep them hidden until the others are ready. We don't want to start a panic around the school so it is imperative that Jesse and Damien keep this quiet." Abraams sounded a little panicky himself.

"My vote is to pull all four of them in today, explain the situation and implore them to keep quiet. They need to prepare themselves mentally for the task ahead of them." Trina coughed and the room became silent. She must have sensed we were there!

I grabbed Damien's arm and guided him to the stairs. We almost made it to the bottom…

"Boys, STOP!" Trina's voice was stern and commanding. We both froze on the stairs and didn't turn around right away. Busted.

"Please find Kyra and Akylas and the four of you join us in Mr. Abraams office immediately." Neither of us said a word and continued down the stairs.

"Well, that was fun." Damien sounded like a 7 year old boy who had been caught throwing a baseball through the kitchen window.

"Let's go." I wanted to get this over with and find out what they knew.

We found Kyra and Akylas together in the courtyard. Damien and I sat at their table taking deep breaths.

"What's up?" Akylas asked, looking a little annoyed that we interrupted their quiet time.

"C'mon, we gotta go. Our mother and brother are in Abraam's office and they want to meet with us." They both looked at me like I just landed from another planet.

"He is serious guys, let's go." Damien said as he stood up and started walking toward the building.

When we arrived at Abraam's office Nikias was gone. *Chicken. He didn't want to face me and own up to the crap he put Mandy and her family through.*

"Wrong, little brother. I'm here, just went to get some tea. I have nothing to apologize for. In fact, you should be thanking me. Mom actually agrees that the less precious Mandy and her family know, the better."

"I'm sorry Jess, but he's right", Trina said. "They have been targeting our kind, their family and friends. All of you please sit down and we'll tell you what we know." Abraam's office was large but we still felt a little cramped with seven of us in there. The four of us sat on his long leather couch, Abraam at his desk. Nikias and Trina took the two leather chairs that sat in front of the desk.

"We're not sure when this began, exactly. We're pretty sure it was a few months before Nikias clumsily brought the two of you here."

Nikias shouted, "Wait, what?! I wanted Damien to be the one to transform Jesse and he did. The whole kidnapping thing just sort of happened. I didn't know TJ would go rogue on me trying to become one of us. It's actually kind of funny if you think about it." If looks could kill, Nikias would be dead from Trina's stare.

"Anyway, Jesse and Damien we brought you here when we did because of the threat to our kind. We weren't sure until a few weeks ago that it was us, our kind, they were targeting. We know there are at least two of our former instructors that went 'rogue', as Nikias so delicately stated, but have not been able to locate them or any others that may be working with them.

We know our computer files have been violated and copied but we didn't discover that until a few weeks ago. So many of our kind have died and some of their innocent family and friends. When we discovered the intrusion to the computers, we removed the files immediately onto flash drives to prevent future tampering. We have been, for lack of a better term, kidnapping our future descendants before these maniacs can kill them.

The island we first brought you to is now filled with future members of our Family who have not been transformed and barely of age. They are of course, scared and freaking out but we had no choice but to pull them way before their time.

We are fairly certain that the traitors figured out we were closing in and have gotten messier. For months they were killing silently and not around large crowds of people; but lately they don't care and as soon as they locate one of us, they implode them where they stand. It's horrible and we have got to figure out who is the mastermind and destroy him! We don't know if it's a civilian or one of us. If it's a civilian then they are hiding him or her well, but once we locate the bastard he or she will be easy to kill. If 'IT' is one of us then we have a tougher task ahead of us.

I feel certain that once we locate the mastermind, then we can bring them all down." Trina took a very deep breath and stared Damien and me in the eyes. She didn't take long before continuing...

"Kyra and Akylas have finished their training and history education on our kind, but you two still have a month to go. We will have to cram four weeks' training into one. We have run out of time and too many innocent people have or are going to die. The caves at the island are at full capacity so we can't bring any more in." She took another deep breath, then Abraams took over the conversation.

"What you and Damien don't know yet is the name of the original family, Matthias. You have not gotten to that part of your schooling." He looked at Kyra and Akylas and they were nodding their heads as they knew the name.

"Even you two do not know this part. The original family is Matthias. Jesse, Damien, Nikias and Trina are that family. All of you are descendants of the original family. We discovered they targeted any of our descendants who had the birthmark but lately they have concentrated on the Matthias side. That is who we 'gathered' at the island. There were only two we could not save but the rest are safe and sound." Kyra and Akylas looked as though they'd seen a ghost and immediately looked over our way.

"So, you see students, you need to work harder! You have to be ready to take on these monsters before they kill more of us." Nikias declared as he paced back and forth.

Trina went on, "What Nikias is trying so gracefully to say, we have to finish your training as quickly as possible. Kyra and

Akylas, we do not want to arouse any suspicion or panic so after graduation tomorrow we will take you two to the island. Jesse and Damien will follow in a few days. We're going to tell any student who questions their early departure that they excelled and tested out. Hopefully that will be enough. We have all the instructors on high alert and have had the shield up around the school for a few weeks. No one, even shape shifters, can get in without Abraams releasing the shield."

"Whoa, shield? What are you talking about?" Akylas asked before any of us could get the words out.

"It is not something we teach, it's just there for protection against any threats, such as the one we're facing now. It's an invisible shield that encompasses the entire school and grounds. No one sees it or can get through. We can't tell you how it works or who knows about it, just know that it is there and you are safe."

"I don't care about the stupid shield. I want to know how Mandy and her family are being protected? Who is behind this mess and why are we still sitting here while these maniacs are killing people?!" I couldn't stand it any longer and was tired of the passive way things were being handled. I'm a cop. I'm used to getting quick results. Nikias looked at Trina…

He asked, "May I?" She nodded her head but glared right through him.

"Because moron, we don't know who is behind it and if we run in blind, it might be us who get killed."

"Killed?! What the hell are you talking about?! According to you, we can't die." By now Nikias and I were standing face to face and if the room were larger I would have phased and taken him. Brother or no brother, I hated him.

"Boys! Sit down, NOW!" Trina stood between us to diffuse the tension, as if that were possible. We stared at each other a minute longer then took our seats, reluctantly.

"Another piece of information we do not teach as this would cause mass killings whenever anger took over, like now. It is true that we are immortal but it is possible to kill us, it's just not a widely known fact." Trina sat back down in her seat and faced the four of us again, trying to stay between Nikias and me.

"I will explain it but I want all of you to understand that if any of this conversation goes outside this room there will be extreme consequences." She waited for the four of us to nod in agreement.

"The only way we can be killed is to pour or spray Hydrofluoric *acid* or (HF) on us. It is quick acting and *will* kill any of us. It is not something just anyone can get their hands on but we are concerned that the traitor or traitors have been teaching the mastermind our secrets. So far, they have concentrated on members of our family who have not transformed yet but we are fearful that they will turn their efforts on those of us who are complete. If it is a civilian or civilians that are behind this, we need to find them quickly and destroy them, then deal with the traitors." Trina took another deep breath and waited for questions. I didn't disappoint.

"Why do you say 'civilians', why not mortals? Isn't that what they call them in the supernatural books and movies?" I knew I was being a smartass, but wanted to ease some of the tension.

"We say civilians as we feel that our Family, or those of us who have completed training and can shape shift are soldiers. It is our job to protect our future shape shifters and those around them, their family and friends. When this current war is over and you return to your normal lives, it will be your job to protect the ones we assign to you until they reach the right age. After you have brought them to us, we assign you new civilians. The job is never ending but very, very important for our survival." Trina stood up and looked at Abraams, who turned to us.

"That's it for now. It's late and tomorrow is a big day. Get some sleep and tomorrow morning after breakfast all four of you meet us here. We'll go over the last details before graduation." He walked around his desk to escort all of us out of his office.

We stood in the hallway after he closed the door with Trina and Nikias still with him.

"Let's get some sleep and see what they have planned tomorrow." Akylas suggested as he and Kyra headed to the stairs.

We returned to the dorm room and got ready for bed. I knew I had to check on Mandy before falling asleep. I lay there trying to get my mind focused on Mandy only. It kept going to the conversation in Abraam's office, then trying to figure out who could be behind this massacre.

It had to be someone with a grudge against The Family, maybe a disgruntled student. Maybe a family member or friend of someone who had transformed and left that person behind. I need to stop and concentrate on Mandy!

Hey get some sleep, you're being too loud. Damien had entered my thoughts and actually yelled at me!

Put your wall up so you don't hear me. I'm trying to find Mandy and make sure she's ok. Maybe you should locate Cassie and make sure she's okay as well.

Not a bad idea. There was silence for a second then we got to work on finding the girls…

> *It didn't take me long, as I knew exactly where to start, the ranch. I concentrated until I was standing between the house and the barn. I stood sideways with my peripheral vision facing both buildings until I heard Mandy's voice. I turned to the barn and waited. There she was, coming out astride a beautiful horse. I didn't know the names of her horses but I knew the ranch was named after her favorite horse, Zamira. Zamira's Dream was an awesome name for a ranch. I stood there in awe and watched her head to the arena. She must not have a class right now as there were no students in the arena.*
>
> *I concentrated a little more and found myself at the arena, sitting on the bleachers watching her work her horse. They were both magnificent. I knew I could watch her without being seen since this was, well, live and not in her dreams. They taught us that we could transfer our*

mind's body to another place without actually being there if we knew the area well enough. We could concentrate hard enough, picturing every detail until we transported our mind's body to that place. We had to be careful though because it weakened us physically and mentally and it would take several minutes to regain all of our strength. I knew I would be fine to do this before going to sleep.

"C'mon Zamira, let's go for a real ride!" Uh, what does that mean? I watched Mandy turn her horse from the middle of the arena and trot to the gate. Wait, she's going to ride off the property! Dang it, how am I going to be with her? I concentrated a little more and wound up behind her on the horse! Cool!! I couldn't feel or smell her but this was the next best thing. Somehow I was able to ride with her on the horse. We rode west of the arena to a trail leading toward the mountain. It was a gorgeous day. Bright blue sky, no clouds and I assumed the air was warm. I couldn't feel that either but I have a good imagination. The mountainside was about a mile or so from the arena so the first part of the trail was flat, but as we neared the looming mountain, the terrain climbed upward.

Before I knew it we were riding through a forest. The trail wound in and out of trees and I found myself ducking my head from tree branches as Mandy did. I laughed to myself when I realized I couldn't get hit by them. We rode for what seemed like hours but it was probably an hour in and out of trees, roots and bushes. I kept looking at her shoulder then down her side to her leg, wishing I could hold her. All of a sudden, we stopped.

"Good boy. Let's get you some water." I looked up to a panorama that took my breath away. We stood at the edge of a clearing full of the most beautiful wild flowers, bordering a lake. The lake was surrounded by majestic mountains. Absolutely breathtaking. She and Zamira stood there for a moment then she edged him to the water. She pulled him to a stop and swung her leg over, right

through me! She hopped off and let him drink from the edge of the lake. I glanced out onto the water and saw ringlets from fish coming up to feed. I couldn't wait until this whole ordeal was over and I could join her here for a real ride.

I listened to the sound of Zamira sucking in water and watched Mandy stroke his neck and mane with her right hand and stare at the lake. It was so peaceful…but not for long. A crackling noise suddenly caught Zamira's attention and he began to side step away from Mandy. His ears were completely upright, head high and snorting. Mandy kept a tight grip on the reins and moved with him trying to calm him down.

"C'mon boy, it's okay. It's probably a deer." She tried to stay calm, but I could tell she was worried. I sat there helpless, frustrated that I couldn't jump down and help her. I concentrated myself to the ground but of course I couldn't grab the reins for her. I had to stand there like an idiot, helpless. All I could do is watch and hope nothing bad happened. Zamira kept pulling on the reins, trying to get further from the sound as he sensed danger.

"Okay boy, if you think it's dangerous, then I trust you. You've never let me down. Let me up and take us away from it." As if Zamira understood what she said, he stood still long enough for her to climb back up. I concentrated myself back up as well.

As soon as Zamira could feel Mandy safely on his back, he wheeled around and thundered back to the trees. Mandy let go of the reins and hugged his neck. I couldn't believe it! She completely trusted this animal's instincts! Is she crazy?! He is going to get her killed!

I decided since I couldn't fall off or get hurt that I would turn myself around and see if a scary deer was chasing us. As I spun around I wished I hadn't! About a hundred yards behind us was a black bear running as fast as his hairy black legs would carry him! We were being chased by a bear! I realized that Zamira knew what he was doing after all and cheered him on. He couldn't hear me but I didn't care, I just kept cheering and yelling.

His hooves pounded the earth, his ears pinned back on his head. I looked down at his shoulder and every muscle quivered as he ran, trying to urge him forward faster and faster. He dodged in and out of the same trees and bushes on the way to the lake and Mandy never sat up to take control of her horse. She trusted him to take her to safety.

As quickly as the danger hit us, it disappeared. I turned to find the bear but he was gone. He must have given up some time ago, thank goodness. Zamira sensed it as well because he slowed his gait and eventually walked.

"Wow! That was amazing! Good boy!!" Mandy hugged him so tight that I thought she would choke him. We walked quietly back to the ranch. When we got closer I saw Tony, her barn manager, outside the barn door.

"Tony, we just encountered a black bear. Keep your eyes peeled. I am going to call Animal Control and have them take it further up the mountain," Mandy yelled from a few yards away.

"Glad you're okay. I'll keep my eyes open, Mandy." He took Zamira after she jumped off. I jumped down as well and decided it was time to return to my temporary world and get some real sleep.

The next morning began like all the others...get up, get dressed, eat breakfast. But instead of heading to classes we met at Abraams' office.

"Everyone sleep well?" Nikias remarked, but he was looking at me.

"What is your problem?"

"I don't have a problem but someone had a little adventure last night." He glared at me but was grinning that 'I know what you did' smirk.

"Stay out of my head!"

"Hey, we need all of you in top condition. I don't want to know what's going on but keep yourselves focused on the battle ahead." Trina pretended to say that to all of us but obviously meant it for Nikias and me. We all took the same positions as the day before on the couch and chairs.

"We decided on a game plan last night after you four left. Kyra and Akylas will go through graduation today. After we leave this office Buzzard will take Jesse and Damien to the island to finish training. Akylas and Kyra will be picked up after graduation. Accelerating Jesse and Damien's training at the school is too risky. Students will become curious and ask too many questions. We are going to have an announcement after graduation that you two have emergencies and will resume training at a later date. None of them will know the difference or think anything of that since they will all have graduated and be gone in a few weeks. The new students will have no idea who any of you are." Abraams actually seemed pleased with himself as he got up to again escort us out.

"You and Damien pack up your belongings and meet Trina in the clearing in an hour. Boys, it's been a pleasure getting to know you and I will see you soon. I will be going to the island as soon as your training is complete, in about a week." He shook our hands and Damien and I headed toward the stairs. We waited for Akylas and Kyra at the bottom of the stairs.

"Congratulations you guys! Wish we could be at graduation but we'll see you in a few hours." They both hugged us and we parted ways.

Damien and I went to the dorm room to pack and tried not to talk to anyone on the way. We both blocked our thoughts so none of the other students could figure out what's going on. I did begin to wonder what made Damien and I, even Nikias, so special. Why did they think we would be able to win this war? Why us? I decided I would ask those questions when we returned to the island.

On the way to the dorm room Adam, our student advisor, walked past us very quickly. He wouldn't look us in the eyes, just stared at the floor.

"Did you see that?" I asked.

"What?"

"Adam, the way he was walking and how fast?"

"Maybe he was late for an appointment with a student." Damien didn't seem concerned so I figured I would forget about it.

We packed our belongings and walked through the courtyard. Sitting at the far end by himself, talking to himself, was Adam. What the heck is going on? Maybe he is aware of everything as well and is nervous that we won't be able to catch the maniacs behind the killings.

I decided to find out, quietly. I grabbed Damien by the arm to make him stop and put my finger to my mouth, hoping he wouldn't say anything. He looked at me like I had lost my mind yet again, but didn't say a word. I pointed to Adam. We dodged behind one of pillars bordering the courtyard so he wouldn't see us spying on him. I put down my barricade and tried to sneak into his head. I hit a brick wall, a thick one. Was he using that to keep out the other students who didn't have a clue? Damien got bored with this and motioned me to continue walking. We were supposed to be at the clearing in ten minutes to meet the elegant Buzzard, who again would take us to our destination.

We walked past Adam, who barely looked up to acknowledge us. I ignored Damien's silent pleas to keep walking and turned toward Adam. I wanted to confront him and I wasn't sure why.

"Hey Adam. How's it going?"

"Fine Jesse, how are you?"

"Good. Are you okay?"

"Yeah, I'm fine. I heard you guys have an emergency and are leaving us temporarily?"

"Yeah, it's not something we can ignore but hopefully we'll be back soon to finish school." I noticed Damien had stayed on the other side of the yard. I didn't know why I would be suspicious of Adam but I wasn't taking any chances at this point. It was probably just the cop in me.

"Well, I hope everything is okay and you return soon. We'll miss you around here." Adam shook my hand and walked into the building.

"Jesse, what is your problem? Let's go!"

"Sheesh, okay. Keep your pants on!"

We arrived above the island and Buzzard dropped us with a subtle thud, not! There is nothing subtle about Buzzard and again he broke my wrist.

"Seriously Buzzard, knock it off! That really hurts!" My wrist popped back into place on its own and was back to normal, but it hurts when it first happens. Buzzard looked at me and I swear he was laughing in his big-clumsy-bird sort of way. He began to flap his giant wings to take off but stopped as quickly as he began. Suddenly another "Buzzard" appeared and landed next to him! You've got to be kidding! Two "Buzzards"? That's just great!

"Actually, there is only one Buzzard but fifteen Ahools which is their scientific name, on the island, dear brother. Buzzard is just the name we gave to your Ahool." Ah, the voice that made me want to chop off my ears. Nikias jumped off the large flying creature.

"Nikias, how many times do I have to tell you to stay out of my head?! And quit calling me 'brother'."

"Why? That's what we are...brothers. Whether you like it or not, brother, we're in this relationship for eternity. Hey, how about a duel before mom gets here? I know you've been itchin to get back at me for messing with your girlfriend." He walked closer to me and his eyes were crimson. I was ready to phase when another "Buzzard" plopped down in the clearing.

"Boys again, knock it off! What are you, five!"

"He started it mom," Nikias sarcastically said, laughing. "Whatever, I'm bored so let's get this show on the road."

"We will Nikki, patience."

"You know I hate it when you call me that."

"I know, and when you can act like a grown-up, I'll go back to your real name."

Ha! Nikki! I love it. Aww Nikki not like his nickname? Come here Nikki. I couldn't help myself.

Go ahead brother. I'll rip you to shreds then watch all your pieces come back together just to rip you up again.

Bring it Nikki! Let's go!

"For Heaven's sake! Let's get settled in and then do a little training before we lose the sunlight." Trina started out of the clearing toward the lake where we would take the boat into the mountainside. There were a lot more people this time than last. All the kids and family members they had saved were roaming around. It was strange. I understood why they had to do it but it seemed cruel.

"Since most of them are still kids are you going to return them to their lives when we catch these bastards?" I had to know.

"That's the plan. Most of them are way too young to transform now. We're hoping this won't take long but unfortunately, we will have to remove their memories of this little adventure before returning them home. I hate doing that but it will be necessary.

I was furious with Nikias when I learned he had removed Mandy and her families' memories. I thought he was just being cruel and wanted to destroy what Mandy and I had. I hated to admit it, but Nikias needed to do it. He didn't have to handle it the way he did though and he should have let me know.

We put our stuff inside the house, got a quick bite to eat then headed out to the training field, which was another boat ride but in the opposite direction. The training field was sort of cool looking. It reminded me of the Police Academy with an obstacle course. Behind the course was a very large field of deep dirt, like a farm field with nothing planted in it. I assumed that was for phasing and fighting, couldn't wait for that.

We stood at the foot of the obstacle course and I took the opportunity to ask some questions before beginning the training.

"Trina, why us? What makes us so special?"

"You *are* special, all three of you. Damien has the analytical, critical thinking we need. You and Nikias, whether you want to admit it or not, have a lot in common. Every generation has at least one who excels in something. Nikias was the first to excel in everything. He took every ability on naturally. Jesse, you did the same. You excelled at anything we threw at you, especially phasing.

Before we start, I need to explain something about what happens when you phase. You may have figured it out already but you hadn't reached that part of the education. When you're in human form you have all your abilities, but not as strong or fast as in the jaguar form. In the jag form you are very strong, agile and fast. You can read each other's minds but can't read civilians' thoughts. You have no invisibility and can't get into civilians' heads or dreams. You also cannot plant visions the way you can in human form.

You have to be careful when in that form. You have human instincts as a jaguar but also have wild instincts. You don't have the desire to kill and eat animals but your natural human instincts are magnified in animal form. For example, if you are naturally inquisitive or suspicious in human form then that will be magnified in jaguar form. That is the case with you, Jesse. As a cop you are naturally suspicious so in jag form you will be very cautious and untrusting of others. In Nikias' case, he is naturally cocky and has anger issues. In jag form he is cockier and angrier. Damien, you are analytical so in jag form you become more so." Trina looked at the ground and we could tell something else was on her mind.

"What are you not saying?" I knew we needed all the facts before heading into the upcoming war.

"There is nothing else. We need to get all of you mentally and physically prepared. We do not know who or what we're dealing with yet. I guess I'm just worried as you and Damien just arrived in my life and I'm sending you into a battle that you may not survive. That thought breaks my heart." A tear rolled down her cheek.

"What makes you think we may not survive? There is only one way for us to die, right? Whoever these monsters are would have to carry spray bottles or whatever holds the acid with them at all times. That would make fighting a little difficult I imagine." I tried to make her feel better but since I wasn't feeling very sensitive these days, that was the best I could do. She did laugh and that broke the ice so we could get on with training.

"Okay, first things first. In a few days there will be a lot more of us coming to the island. We have gathered the best and strongest. One of them will be here tomorrow and he will be doing the training with you and Damien that was missed at school. Nikias will be working with Akylas and Kyra, who should be here any time. We have a couple hours of daylight so I'll work with you two now." Nikias was running through the obstacle course while we got the pep talk. Trina turned her attention to him.

"Go wait for the other two and bring them here as soon as they arrive. They can put their stuff away after training."

"Aye, aye captain." Nikias said as he rolled his eyes. Trina shook her head and returned to Damien and me.

"Damien, tomorrow I would like you to work with Kyra and see if you can figure out who is behind these killings. Kyra is excellent with dissecting and piecing together problems. With both your brains working on this, maybe you can 'find' him/her or them. We're placing the two of you in the field but you will be our eyes and ears only. We want you two to put your strengths together and locate these bastards. I will let you know in a couple of days where you will be staying. It will be somewhere in the United States as most of the family is there. We have people protecting the ones who are abroad." She backed up a couple of steps and looked at both of us.

"Remember, we are not dealing with civilians alone. We are dealing with our own kind, which will make this ordeal a lot more complicated. I have been hoping and praying that the traitors have not tried to transform the monster mastermind. If we can get to the monster first, our jobs will be a little easier."

"If they did 'transform' him or her, isn't there a chance that they wouldn't survive?" I could tell Damien was already putting his critical thinking cap on.

"Absolutely but since there were two more killed just last night in Oklahoma, we're pretty sure it hasn't happened yet. If it had, the civilian who was transformed would be sloppy for several weeks and make mistakes, let their guard down so we could swoop in and 'find' him or her. Even with the help of our traitors they would not be able to control how the civilian thinks. Jesse, you remember how random and careless your thoughts were for awhile when Damien was 'finding' and transforming you?"

"Yeah but I had no clue what was happening. I would think that if I was behind something like this and knew how imperative it was to conceal my identity, I would be able to control my thoughts and keep up walls."

"Good point but no matter the motivation, the transformation takes over and carelessness is inevitable, especially for the first few days. We have had people 'monitoring' random thoughts pretty much 24/7. When there are killings, they concentrate in that area. They have a list of remaining family members who are still out there, ones we don't have room for at the island. They are monitoring their every move."

"Who is doing the monitoring and placing us around the world?"

"You met one of them your first day at the school. It's your advisor, Adam. He is doing a good job trying to keep things under wraps at school and protecting those we can't but they still stay a step ahead of us. That is why we need more resources out there and need to get all of you in the field. We have pulled everyone and every resource we have, yet they're still killing. He will be coming out here in a few days to do the final briefing on all of your locations."

"Are you sure you can trust him? How do you know he is not a traitor and stayed on the inside to move their mission along? It actually makes a lot of sense and when I saw him yesterday, he was acting very strange." My gut had been telling me not to trust him.

"I know we can trust him; he was acting strange because he had just found out about the killings in Oklahoma. It's driving him crazy. He says he puts his walls up and makes them solid but somehow they are still getting in and finding the ones we protect." Just then, Nikias, Kyra and Akylas came strolling up the path to join us.

"Hi again!" Kyra seemed light hearted. I'd never seen her that way, in fact, she was skipping!

"Hey, how was graduation? Wish I could've seen you in cap and gowns."

"No cap and gowns just typical ceremony, blah, blah, blah. Glad it's over cause I'm ready to kick some ass!" Akylas was his usual self and I was happy for that since we would need all kinds of attitude out there.

Trina resumed, "All right everyone, let's get to work! Nikias, take Kyra and Akylas to the field and work with them on phasing and fighting. Go over things they have already learned and fine tune them. Kyra, since you missed some of the conversation earlier I'll explain what your job will be after training tonight." Kyra nodded her head at Trina and went with Nikias.

"Jesse and Damien, you two will stay with me. We will go over some of the points you would have learned these last few weeks at school. The next four days will be rough but crucial. We will cram those last four weeks into four days. I'm sorry it has to be this way."

"It's okay, let's get started." I was also ready to kick some ass!

"One of the things that I don't think they emphasized yet is what happens when you have a vision or when one is planted in your head. You have to know the difference as that will slow you down and confuse situations. That could get you killed because you're concentrating on the vision and see nothing else, your defenses are down. Our traitors will know that and it's easy to plant anything into someone's head, us or civilians.

A vision will always make your head pound. That is the only thing that will hurt your head but is it real or planted? Determining that can be the difference between surviving or possible death. Reading thoughts or talking with your mind will not hurt. Going into someone's dreams will not hurt. But going into dreams or entering their heads while they're awake, will lower your strength for a few minutes. Use those abilities wisely and when you know you have a few minutes to regain your strength. Jesse, it was amazing to me that you found your abilities so naturally after Damien transplanted them.

Nikias had been keeping an 'eye' on all of you and told me what had happened. You naturally found invisibility and all the other ones without any training. Honestly, I think that is another reason he picks on you. There may be a little jealousy there."

I heard that! I'm NOT jealous of that moron!

Bring it Nikki, I'm right here!

Oh, we'll have our day little brother!!

"Sometimes I wish we couldn't hear each other's thoughts! It's really annoying..." Trina's voice trailed off and my head started pounding...

> *It was Mandy, sitting in a church among a lot of people dressed in black. She had her hands over her face, crying.*
>
> *"Why did you have to fight Jesse?! You could have stayed with me and you'd still be alive!"*
>
> *The teenager I saw in her house a few days ago had her arm around Mandy and was hugging her tight.*

"C'mon Mandy let's go." Her secretary/friend, Becca came to the edge of the pew and urged Mandy to go with her.

I tried calling to her but she didn't see or hear me. Why did she think I was dead? I'm right here! I looked at the front of the church...a casket. I walked up to it and looked inside...there I was! My arms folded over my chest, dressed in a black suit, eyes closed. Wait, that can't be me! I can't die like a normal person. No way would I look like that!...

"Jesse. JESSE! Get up." Trina had her hand on my shoulders and was shaking me violently. I started gathering my senses and heard Nikias laughing from the other side of the field!

"You son of a...!!!" I got up and ignored the pleading sounds from Trina. I couldn't take it any longer, this had been a long time coming. I ran and felt my body changing, expanding and screaming for my other form. My other senses; vision and hearing instantly magnified. It always felt like minutes for this change to happen, but was only a second. I had four legs now and all moved in sync faster and faster toward my mortal enemy who had also phased instantly. I saw in my peripheral vision that Akylas and Kyra had stepped to the side. So far, Trina wasn't interfering either. Good, let us at each other!

Nikias stood his ground in jag form, eyes crimson and muscles tense. I slammed to a stop on all fours, inches from his nose. Dirt had flown up around him and landed on his back but he didn't move a muscle.

Bring it little brother! You know I will take you in an instant!

I blocked off my thoughts and said nothing. We stayed nose to nose glaring into each other's eyes. I guess Nikias was bored with that...

What's the matter, scared that I'll take over where you left off with Mandy when you're dead and gone?

That did it! I reared up on my hind legs and came down over his face with my right front paw, claws stretched out to full capacity. Blood trickled down his snout. I could feel rage pulsing through my entire body and Mandy's face stayed in my mind the whole time. Nikias backed up two steps then reared on his hind legs. I went under him and grabbed his right back leg with my teeth. He grunted at the pain and came down on my hindquarters, both his front legs straddling either side, digging his claws into my back legs.

We both retreated then, and came at each other from the front. Dirt was flying overhead, landing in our eyes and mouths. I went for him again and wrapped my front legs around his neck and bit his shoulder as hard as I could. He whipped his neck around and bit my shoulder. Both of us writhed in pain, but didn't let that stop us. My back paws clung to the dirt to hold my ground but he lunged forward and I lost my balance. I fell over onto my back and he took advantage by pouncing on top of me, digging his large canine teeth into my jugular. For a few seconds I couldn't breathe. I managed to get all four legs under him and, all my strength, tossed him off me like a rag doll. I leapt back to my using feet and went after him again. He scrambled to regain his balance, his body twisted with back half lying on the ground and the front half about to get up.

I lunged at his front left shoulder and pushed him back down. I kept my front left paw and claws into his neck to keep him down. I dug my teeth into his shoulder while my right paw held his hindquarters down. I finally had him! He couldn't move. I felt like I could kill him at this instant - if we could die. At the very least, tear him to pieces. As angry and full of rage as I felt at this creature, I couldn't continue. My humanity returned and my body retreated, phasing me back.

I was back in human form but Nikias remained a jaguar and lay still on the ground. I figured I had hurt him pretty badly and his body was healing. I turned to the little man that brought my clothes when suddenlyTrina screamed. I looked at her, not sure what she said. She had phased and was running full speed toward us! As I turned back to Nikias, he had gotten up and eyes wild with rage, lunged at me...while I was still human! I don't know how I did it with this creature on top of me but I phased back to jag form while under Nikias! By this point he had his teeth buried in the back of my neck. I stood up, half of him on top of me then twisted my entire body to the ground to rub him off. I got up and grabbed his chest with my teeth and planted all four feet firmly to the ground so he couldn't knock me over. He tried but failed. He brought up his right front paw and latched it onto my left shoulder. I released my grip on his chest and we both reared up again.

As we both came down, Trina got between us and reared up, knocking both of us off balance. We fell on our sides, phased back to human form and grabbed the clothes brought to us by our helpers.

Trina seethed, "Is it finally out of your systems?! I can't take this any longer. You two are brothers whether you like it or not and have bigger problems to deal with than your egos! You have successfully wasted the rest of this day so we'll have to work that much harder the next few days." She stormed off and returned to Damien, who by now was sitting with Kyra and Akylas by the obstacle course. Guess they didn't want to get dirt and blood all over themselves, can't blame them for that.

I turned to Nikias and we glared at each other for a few seconds.

"Quit messing with my head! Why would you want to mess with someone as innocent as Mandy? What's your problem?" Nikias kept glaring, but then his eyes turned soft.

"You make it easy. I know your weakness and I go for it. That's exactly what these maniacs will do, I guarantee it. You don't keep your wall up to hide your weaknesses or emotions. It will take one second for them to see Mandy's face in your brain and that's all she wrote, you belong to them. You let my fake vision in, even though you knew what it meant, your strength would be diminished. All your defenses went up in smoke. You became vulnerable and if I had been one of the real monsters, I would have killed you with the acid I had ready. But whatever, it won't break my heart if those idiots get hold of you." He walked toward the others. I really hated to admit it but he made a lot of sense. I would never admit that to him though.

The next morning we all met at the training field. There was still tension between Nikias and me but not as bad. Trina hadn't shown up yet so Akylas, Nikias and I started training on the obstacle course. Kyra and Damien had brought a pad of paper and pencils and decided to strategize on the picnic table located east of the obstacle course.

Trina came walking up the path but wasn't alone.

"Zander?!" Akylas jumped off the wooden wall we had been climbing and ran to the stranger, throwing his arms around him in a hug.

"Who is Zander?" I actually directed a normal question to Nikias and after the words came out, I was surprised. When I glanced at Nikias, who hadn't answered me, looked as if he'd seen a ghost.

"His older brother." He jumped down and just stared.

"That's pretty cool. Why do you look as though this is not good news?"

"It's fine, I just didn't know he'd be here." I looked back at Akylas who was hugging his brother. Zander hugged him back but stared at Nikias. He released his grip from Akylas and headed our way.

"Zander."

"Nikias." They looked each other up and down, then Zander turned to Akylas again.

"How you been little brother?"

"Good. Getting ready to kick some ass! Is that why you're here?"

"Yep, and to keep an eye on my little brother." Zander rubbed the top of Akylas' head and glared at Nikias once more. They stood there, staring each other down.

"Why do they look like they're about to kill each other? Don't get me wrong, I'd love it if Zander made Nikias beg for mercy." I directed the question and comment to Trina, who never let me down with answers.

"They have history." I take it back, she did let me down.

"Well, that was cryptic." That's all she would say, really?

"I'll tell ya the story." Akylas spoke up, put his arm around my shoulder and guided me to a patch of grass to take a seat.

"Remember when I told you Nikias saved my brother's life?"

"I forgot about that. Which was why you couldn't see the jerk Nikias really is. You saw him as a saint." I belted out a pretend laugh but Akylas didn't get the joke.

"Zander was living in Chicago when Nikias grabbed him and took him to the school. One of them will have to tell you the whole story - but the short version is, my brother was being mugged by two thugs who were beating the crap out of him. Nikias showed up just in time, pounded the thugs and got Zander out of there.

Zander and I are three years apart and were always close until he and my parents got into a big fight when he was 17. My family lives in Peoria, Illinois but Zander moved to Chicago when they got into that fight. I hadn't seen him again until he graduated from this school. He came back home after five years and tried repairing the damage with my parents. They still haven't forgiven him but Zander swore he and I would stay close." Akylas' eyes began to tear up. He shook it off and continued.

"Zander explained the whole story, which of course I didn't believe. He made me take off my shoes and socks and look at the bottom of my feet, we had the same birthmark. I still thought he was insane so he took me out to a vacant lot in the middle of nowhere and showed me his abilities. If I had had a sensitive stomach, I would have thrown up.

I'm still not sure what happened later between Nikias and Zander but I know it had to do with a girl. I have no idea who or what happened.

Three years later Nikias grabbed me and the rest, as they say, is history." Akylas was smiling by the end of that story, another first for me to witness.

The next few days were filled with fighting, phasing, invisibility, climbing, crawling and mind games. The ones training us focused a lot on making our mind defenses strong so none of our enemies could penetrate. Our senses and bodies were as sharp as they were going to get. We were ready!

Damien and Kyra had been working day and night trying to get a sense of the swine behind these horrific killings. Trina, school officials and instructors could only identify two of the traitors. They knew there must be many. The head swine, as Kyra liked to call him, was buried deep underground and had been trained well to hide himself. Trina had 'seen' the two traitors a couple times but they quickly disappeared from her sight. She had given each of us pictures of these two to burn into our minds.

By the end of the week there were 150 more 'soldiers' who had joined the ranks on the island. Every one of them was a graduate and had been living normal lives for years. The oldest one was 200 years old! His name was Nicos. He had some interesting stories but he said this was the worst threat to our kind he had ever witnessed. 'We protect them from their own kind. We've never had one of them attack us!' It was unsettling to see a 200 year old man look like the rest of us and have the same strengths, abilities and sharp senses.

Nicos also told us stories of his father that dated back to the beginning, the 16th Century. He explained how exciting it was when the school was formed 200 years ago. He was in the first graduating class. Before the school opened, they trained the new ones the best way they could, but it was unorganized and sloppy. So much information was lost in translation and most never understood their full potential. He laughed and said they probably still don't know their full potential.

We all were leaving in two days to take our posts and start the searches, but tonight Trina wanted to give us a night off to have some fun. We made a huge bonfire in the middle of the training field, drank beer and ate lots of food. We had fighting matches which were really interesting. There were times when more than 100 huge jaguars of all different colors - black, spotted, black fading into spots, were all running around play-fighting and tearing up the obstacle course.

I was play fighting with Damien when, out of the corner of my eye, I saw Trina walking up to someone. It was Adam. A few of the newcomers stopped what they were doing and ran up to him.

"Hey Adam, long time no see!" Nicos was the first to reach him next to Trina.

"Hi Nicos. It has been a very long time. In fact, I think the last time I saw you was about 50 years ago when you came to the school to speak to the students. You're looking good for a two-hundred year old man." They both laughed and hugged each other. Nicos was a tall muscular man, about 6'3" and probably 230 pounds., all muscle. Adam looked like an ant compared to Nicos.

"Okay Adam, let's go to the house and strategize before our meeting with everyone tomorrow. Fill me in on your plan." They walked off and everyone continued partying. Good thing we would have two days to recuperate, we would all need it.

A couple of hours later things died down and people started finding places to sleep. Some stayed in jag form and slept in trees, some curled up under trees and rested on tree trunks. The four of us went to the house. Damien, Akylas and Kyra headed upstairs and I told them I would be up in a minute. Damien went up last, but stood on the bottom stair looking me. He didn't want to say anything out loud or in his brain as he could tell I was in detective mode. I gave him the 'go ahead, it's okay' look and he left, shaking his head.

I heard Trina, Nikias and Adam talking in the den so I walked quietly to the kitchen, right next door. I figured if I was busted I could grab a glass and pretend to get some water. I had my walls up in my head so no one could 'hear' or sense me. Nikias and Trina had their defenses down so it was easy to get into their heads, but those weren't the brains I wanted to investigate. I jumped over to Adam's and he still had his guard up. Why? He didn't have to hide from anyone here right? I lingered a few minutes more, then headed upstairs.

The next morning breakfast was waiting for everyone outside. I didn't even want to think about who cooked it and how early they must have gotten up to prepare breakfast for hundreds of people. That was too much for my brain before coffee.

After breakfast, Trina had a group of us help position some bleachers in the training field and get a podium set up with a microphone for Adam. There were not enough bleachers so we let the ladies take the seats and the guys found places on the dirt. There were hundreds of different conversations, whispering and mumbling going on before Adam started for the podium. Trina stood next to him near a long table that held a stack of papers.

"Can I have everyone's attention please?" Adam tapped the mic once before speaking and it squealed very loudly. That was enough to get our attention. Everyone quieted immediately.

"Thank you - sorry for the ear piercing noise. I want to go over the next steps of the plan, then Trina will hand out papers to everyone with your individual itineraries. It's very important that everyone stick to the itinerary so we can monitor what's going on and keep everyone safe. Trina has already briefed everyone but I will give you some facts that will help with this mission..."

His voice faded as I watched him and tried to get into his brain. I didn't think he would have anything to say that Trina had not told the four of us already. Damien was sitting to my right and I noticed his attention was on me, not in an obvious sort of way, but in a blank stare sort of way. I ignored it and concentrated solely on Adam. It seemed that the harder I concentrated, the more solid his wall became. He couldn't know I was trying to get in, could he? Nah, no way. I decided to wait until tonight when he fell asleep. It's possible for us to keep our guard up when we're sleeping, but not many of us can.

He spoke for about an hour and then answered questions. When he finished, Trina called out names and had everyone come and get their itineraries. That lasted another hour or so.

"All right everyone, that about does it. You can relax the rest of the day but get plenty of sleep tonight. In the morning, Buzzard and his buddies will take everyone in shifts. They can each take eight of you at a time and there are fifteen of them, you do the math. There will be three separate shifts and listed on your itinerary is your shift and approximate time you will leave. If you're on the first shift, have your belongings and yourself in the training field at 6 a.m. You will leave by 6:15. The other two shifts, be here at least 15 minutes before your bird is scheduled to leave.

Me, Nikias, Kyra, Damien, Akylas and Zander were in the second shift. So we needed to be in the field by noon. We compared itineraries and they had all of us going to Phoenix, Arizona. That wasn't bad, I didn't mind heading in that direction. I knew I wouldn't be able to make a side trip until this whole mess was over but if it kept Mandy and her family safe, I would wait.

The rest of the day was long. Most slept off their hangovers and those of us who didn't drink very much, kept busy. Some read, some trained...I kept close tabs on Adam. Since he had his walls up I couldn't 'watch' him with my mind or get into his head, so I followed him most of the day. A couple of times he almost caught me but luckily there are many trees so I was able to zig and zag to safety. I followed all day but still, nothing. So far, he seemed on the straight and narrow but I just couldn't shake the feeling he knew something.

He didn't move around very much, most of the day was spent in the house reading. He would get up from time to time and mingle outside with everyone. It still bothered me that around all of us he kept those walls up. Why? Supposedly, he had them up at school to keep the students out and not cause a panic but around us he wouldn't have needed the walls. He was definitely hiding something and I decided I wouldn't stop until I uncovered it.

Nightfall rolled in with a full moon and a billion twinkling stars. The air was a cool and crisp. People began to migrate to their resting areas, saying good night to all their newfound friends. The four of us again headed to the house. I decided not to tell Damien my theory as he tends to be careless with his thoughts. I didn't want to endanger him or blow my cover. I told them I was not tired and would be up later. I sat in the den and pretended to read. As I predicted, Adam came strolling by and we said good night to each other. I pretended to continue reading in case he looked back at me. I would wait a little while then attempt his thoughts again.

"Not tired?" Trina interrupted my thought process.

"No. I'm a little anxious so I decided to read, but it's not calming me down. What about you?" I hadn't even thought of what she might be going through. She was sending her three boys off to war.

"Me too. I'm worried, but I am so proud of all you. I wish I could have raised all of you. I think of how different our lives would have been. I'm relieved though that one of my boys had a great set of parents." Her thoughts were random but I understood how she felt. I wished we could have grown up together as one big happy family as well, but I was thankful I had a great childhood. I felt bad for Damien and even a little sad for Nikias, well maybe not Nikki.

"We'll be okay, Trina. When this is all over; you, me, Damien, Kyra, Akylas, Zander, Mandy, Cassie and even Nikias will all meet in St. Thomas, and we'll have the vacation that was stolen from us. I think you owe us that much." I laughed and winked at her before giving her a hug. She hugged me tight and we said good night.

I waited about an hour and let everyone fall asleep - especially Adam. I crept upstairs and sat outside his room in the hallway. Just as I suspected, he couldn't keep his wall up when sleeping. Good job Adam.

Strange images were swirling around in his brain and partial sentences that made no sense, but I kept 'listening' and 'watching'. Two hours later I was getting frustrated wondering if I may have been wrong and there was nothing to worry about with him. But then...a face of someone I had never seen before, but was oddly familiar, appeared in his thoughts. I kept my distance so I wouldn't disturb Adam's slumber but I concentrated harder. He was in a deep sleep and his thoughts and images started turning into dreams. This would be tricky now, because I needed to stay 'outside' his dreams but still needed to 'hear' and 'see' what was going on.

The face gradually became a body and it was lying down on some sort of bed. I couldn't tell where this dream took place. It was dark and dingy, yet some sort of light illuminated the room. A cave, a lantern? The images were fading in and out.

A shadow appeared close to this man but I couldn't tell who or what it was. There was no sound except the quiet breathing of the man lying down. Then I heard Adam's voice!

> *"Sebastian don't wake up, just listen. I have to make this quick but I have all the itineraries and I will get them to you the usual way. It has all the names and locations of everyone. They are all leaving tomorrow and by nightfall they'll be settled in their positions."*
>
> *"Good. Get the itineraries to me first thing in the morning and I will have our people positioned and ready for all of their arrivals. When the last one has left, grab*

Trina and bring her to me. Finally, my revenge is close. Now go!" The man on the bed opened his eyes and sat up.

Oh my God, Adam really is a traitor! I got a good look at the man but still had no clue as to his identity - and what does want with Trina? Damn, I realized I said all of that in my head but with no wall up! I put up my defense and sat quietly, making sure Adam didn't 'hear' me. Whew, I don't think he did. As long as he didn't suspect me, he would have no reason to get into my head. I had to keep it that way.

I went to our room and Damien was also in a deep sleep. I decided it would be safer to enter his dream and tell him my discovery instead of waiting until morning and risk Adam hearing us. I climbed into my bed and closed my eyes. I was anxious and had to force myself to relax and concentrate on Damien...

I'm in. Who knows what he dreams but I was about to find out. I stood in the middle of blackness at first. Words and images spun around me but I forced myself to stand still and tried not to get dizzy. Then I saw him. The blackness turned to sunshine and we were on a beach. He was sitting on a blanket and there was a girl with him. Aw, how sweet, it's Cassie! I was pretty sure it was his dream and not Cassie's.

I walked up to the blanket.

"Damien. I'm sorry to interrupt this beautiful moment but I have to tell you something, now."

"Get out of my head! I'll talk to you in the morning!"

"It can't wait. I found out Adam is a traitor and I have an image of the man who is behind it all. Damien, look at me!" Cassie disappeared and Damien turned around on his blanket.

"This better be good!"

"It is but I can't figure out who the man is or where he is hiding. I've got the man's face in my head and I want you to 'look' at him. Concentrate Damien, you can do

this." Damien closed his dream eyes and in a minute or so
his eyes shot open in his dream and he woke up!

When he woke up it felt like I was shot through a cannon and I opened my eyes.

"Don't do that! You scared the crap out of me! Did you recognize the man in my head?" Damien was white as a ghost and shook violently.

"That can't be the man! You have the wrong image in your head." He got out of bed and paced the floor.

"I don't have it wrong, it's burned in my brain. He told Adam to get our itineraries to him, and then when we have all left he wants Adam to grab Trina and bring her to him. He wants revenge on her for something." I got up and grabbed him by the arm.

"Stop pacing and talk to me. Who is this man?" He stopped, turned to face me but was still white as a ghost and tried to speak. It sounded like he had sand in his throat.

"Our father – that's our demon father! That's why I tell you that you're wrong! That s.o.b. is dead and living in Hell. There is no way The Family would have let him live. They wouldn't have lied to Trina about that."

"Well, let's think this through. First of all, did he have a brother?"

"Not that I know of. And anyway, it would have to be an identical twin because that ugly monster looks just like him!"

"Let's wake up Trina and fill her in. Maybe he does have a twin no one knows about, or maybe she knows him. Maybe she would know why this creep has a vendetta against her. Let's go, but be quiet. We can't let Adam know that we have figured part of this out." Trina's room was at the end of the hall and Nikias' was next to hers. We quietly woke them both up and told them to meet us in the field.

Nikias was furious. "What the hell is going on! This better be good or I'm whipping you again Jesse!"

"Shut up, Nikias, and listen." We sat them down on the bleachers and told them everything I saw and heard. The looks on their faces were the same as Damien's. Trina actually turned whiter than Damien had, and if she hadn't been sitting, she would have fallen down.

"You have to be mistaken. He is dead."

"Trina, I showed you the image and that came straight from Adam's head. I never knew Petros, thank goodness, and I have never seen pictures of him. This can't be wrong. Did Petros have an identical twin?" I took her hands in mine to calm her down, but she was shaking so hard I could barely hold them. She got up and started pacing like Damien. They sure have the same genes.

"He does." My heart fell into my stomach and pounded so loudly I worried that Adam may even hear it.

"He's been in prison for murder since, well, before I met Petros. He was sentenced to life without parole for murdering his best friend. He found him in bed with his wife and shot both of them. His friend died and his wife is paralyzed from the neck down and as far as I know, she's still in an institution. The Family kept tabs on Sebastian - that's his name - for years. A few years after I was rescued, they stopped monitoring him. I guess that was a big mistake. But how can this be? How did he get out of prison? Why would he be after me? I never met the man…" The wheels started turning in her head as her sentence trailed off. She stopped pacing and started thinking. I wanted to jump into her thoughts but stayed out of it.

"What is it?" Nikias had been sitting quietly the whole time, letting it all sink in.

"This is really grasping at straws but it's the only thing that makes sense. Go with me on this while I think out loud. Petros was killed by our Family and his brother is rotting in prison. A friend of Petros goes to the prison to tell him his brother has been killed. Who is to blame for his brother's death, me.

The only thing to do in prison is think and research. What if Sebastian figured everything out about the Family somehow? He has the knowledge and starts screaming in his head to any of us that will listen. He finds one of our kind who visits him and a plan is born? He escapes prison and forms an army to kill off the future Family members and leaves the best for last...me." She takes a deep breath and stood in front of us for a minute. We all stayed silent while processing.

Nikias sat up straighter in his chair. "Okay, let's assume this is true. What does he have to offer our kind that they would betray us?"

Trina replied, "I didn't say I had the whole thing figured out, just a theory at this point. Before we go any further we have to deal with Adam. We have to find a way to detain and silence him before morning and he releases the itineraries. That's the first thing on the agenda."

Nikias jumped up. "Wait. Jesse couldn't tell where this maniac is hiding, right? Even with the image in his head, he can picture him but if this creep never leaves the hiding place, we won't be able to see any landmarks to pinpoint his location. We need Adam to lead us to him. What if we make up fake itineraries and Adam delivers them? How was he going to deliver them?" Nikias looked straight at me with that question of course.

I replied, "He just told the guy he would get them to him the usual way, whatever that means."

"Good, that's okay. I'm sure Adam did not memorize the itineraries, he has no reason to. He's leaving the dirty work to this jackass and our traitors in the field. Let's give the man what he wants - only it will be completely wrong. We'll send all of them on a wild goose chase while we close in on the snake's den. While they're running around like chickens with their heads cut off, Jesse will get into this creep's head and start freaking him out. All of his guards, for lack of a better term, will be hunting all of us.

Jesse will flush him out of hiding,then we swoop in and destroy him." He had another thought that he knew Trina would not like. He looked at her, and she must have read his mind.

"I know Nikias. I already thought of that."

Now I jumped in. "What? What are you not telling us?"

"After Adam gives the fake information and contacts this jerk one more time then we're going to have to kill him. We need him a little longer so suspicion isn't raised - but then we have to quiet him for good."

"Oh, that makes sense." Damien said and I could tell he felt bad for Trina. She really despised violence but when it comes to war, it's sometimes necessary.

"We will keep this information between us and everyone go to their assigned posts. However, we will tell Akylas and Kyra in the morning. When you're scheduled time arrives at noon we will have Buzzard take all of you to the other side of the island so Adam thinks you're gone. I will let you know when the coast is clear and he will bring you back."

I had a thought. "Wait a minute. How will we keep track of Adam? When he is awake he has the Berlin Wall going on up there. We have to find a way to follow or go with him to deliver the itineraries." I was not going to let that weasel slip out of our hands. Trina paced back and forth a few minutes before coming up with an alternate plan.

"Hmm...then Buzzard will pretend to fly off with all of you becoming invisible but he will only take you to the end of the training field. Adam's bird will be picking him up in the field at 4:00. All of you have got to have your minds stronger and more solid than ever. If Adam doesn't penetrate any of your thoughts then he will probably return to school after he's dropped off the itineraries. We can keep tabs on him there until we have all the traitors and Sebastian taken care of."

"What happens after he delivers the itineraries? Do we go to our posts?" Damien asked with a very worried look on his face.

Trina seemed to mull this over. "Let's think this through. He delivers the itineraries, then you six follow the person or persons to the assigned area. Hopefully he, she or they will immediately deliver the papers and you can take care of the snake's head on the spot. No, that won't work because if the gofers who deliver the papers get away, they will warn all the other traitors out in the field." Trina had a good point but I thought if we were armed we could handle it.

"How about this...we go armed with acid. At the most there will be two delivery weasels and between the six of us we can take on all of them. Then we find the other traitors and take care of them." I thought I had a foolproof plan but Damien had doubts.

"How do we keep the acid rifles invisible? We can't turn inanimate objects invisible."

"Damien, are you on drugs?! What about your clothes? They become invisible when you do. Anything on our body will be invisible." Aww, I knew Nikias wouldn't let us down with his sarcasm.

"Okay, I didn't think about that, smart ass." The two of them glared at each other.

"This is what I worry about. The tension between the three of you is going to get you killed! When you're angry and fighting your mind defenses go away. I wouldn't be surprised if Adam hasn't already heard everything." Trina was up and pacing again.

"No, forget all of it! It's me they want and it will be me they get. I can't let anyone else die. We are looking at this from the wrong angle. We use Sebastian's anger as a weapon and draw him and all the traitors out into the open."

"NO! Mom, you are not doing this! I won't allow it!" Nikias' eyes turned crimson and Damien and I backed up a step.

Trina continued, "Settle down, Nikias. Think about it. We somehow imitate Adam's voice and talk to this monster, pretending to be Adam. We tell him that he needs to gather all the gofers at the cave, or wherever he is, to strategize since the other army – us - are in place. Still pretending to be Adam, we tell him that he will be bringing me to the gathering. We send our people away with the real itineraries, give Sebastian fake ones then when they are all gathered, we pounce. It will work."

"Maybe. As long as you don't go out there alone."

"I'm not suicidal, Nikias. We will all go out together."

"Okay then, let's get to work." Nikias was as anxious as the rest of us to put a stop to these monsters. I looked at Damien to make sure his wall was solid. I tried peeking in and he had a good defense in his brain.

It didn't take long for Trina to change the itineraries on the computer and print the copies for Adam. Luckily, Adam trusted everyone and his duffel bag was sitting on the floor in the den. I replaced the real itineraries with the fake ones. By now, it was one in the morning so we decided to go to bed. We would meet at six in the field, pretend all is well, then take Akylas and Kyra aside. We would write everything down and tell them to keep walls up while they're reading so Adam wouldn't find out.

Trying to fool others of our kind is very tricky. If Adam suspected for a second we were on to him he would 'peek' into all of our brains and the jig would be up.

I lay in bed tossing and turning. I had my defense up and kept my thoughts inside the wall. I knew there had to be a better way. I decided to concentrate on the image of Sebastian. Depending on his location, it might be daylight and he may be awake. Maybe he would put his defenses down enough for me to pinpoint his location. I concentrated but kept my distance so he wouldn't 'see' me...

It didn't take long to find him. It was definitely some sort of cave. It was daylight now and he was sitting up on his cot. He looked anxious and kept looking at his watch. I'm sure he was waiting to hear from Adam. I stayed quietly in his head but I was on the outside of a wall. His concentrated thoughts remained inside so he had no clue I was there.

I then realized I wasn't alone...Nikias appeared! He obviously had the same idea and we gave each other a glare, then without saying a word, nodded and worked together.

Sebastian needs to step outside. C'mon, you need some Vitamin D. He did it! We started moving and the light got brighter. Nikias and I turned around with our backs against his wall watched through Sebastian's eyes. He stepped to the lip of the cave and I could tell it was at a lower elevation, not high in a mountain. He was in shorts and a t-shirt so I'm thinking, desert maybe? It was rocky to about 50 feet outside the cave then sand as far as I could see. Sebastian had been pacing the entrance of the cave, back and forth. He couldn't be waiting for Adam's itineraries yet, way too early for that. He must be waiting...

Nikias nudged my arm and he was looking to the left. I glanced the same direction and bingo! One of Sebastian's lackeys was walking toward him! Yes! I looked at Nikias and he was turning colors of green then white. He must have recognized this guy. The brute stood about 6 foot, military style hair cut and had muscles coming out of his muscles! He carried a large wooden crate. They spoke to each other but we couldn't hear, they both had their walls up. I looked at Nikias again and his color had returned but his eyes were crimson! Whoa, can we phase in someone's head?! No way! I nudged his arm this time and gave him the 'you better calm down' look. He would blow our cover!

The guy brought the crate into the cave and pried it open with a hammer. Supplies! Of course! I hadn't considered that people have to bring him food and necessary supplies. Not sure yet, but that may help. I was excited and looked at Nikias, he was gone! What the?...

> *I stayed in Sebastian's head and decided not to worry about what Nikias was up to. Unfortunately, Sebastian was very boring. He pulled out some packets of some kind of food from the crate after Mr. Brute left and started eating. The chewing and crunching noises were disgusting. I turned around to his wall and was just about to leave when Nikki showed up again. He motioned for me to leave with him and looked very excited.*

We jumped out of Sebastian's head and back to reality. I got up quietly and looked down the hall - nothing. Where is Nikias?

"*Field.*" That was all he needed to say. I hurried and joined him out there and he looked as though he was jumping out of his skin. He had a piece of paper that started with 'keep your walls up while you read'. Then the rest of it…

> *I know exactly where Sebastian is! I also know how many are in their army, only 42! They already have a plan to meet at the cave to strategize! In two days at 1 p.m. We will be there with acid rifles in hand and with a surprise attack we can take them all at once. They won't know what hit them with over 150 of us!!!*

Then I wrote…

Get Trina and the others quietly and meet at the field.

I grabbed the note and left for the field. Nikias gathered everyone, including Akylas, Kyra and Zander this time and met me by the bleachers.

We first showed Trina the note, then filled in the others. Everyone had good defenses in place so Adam couldn't 'hear'. The only obstacle was how to fake getting everyone off the island. Adam had to think everyone in our army was heading to their posts shown on the itineraries. In reality, they would all stay here, on the island. How would we tell 150 people what's going on without Adam 'hearing'? We all put our brains into hyper think mode while keeping our walls up! Not an easy task. Finally Akylas came up with a simple plan...

"Trina, can you get a bunch of blank paper and 7 pencils or pens and bring them here?" Trina ran to the house to retrieve the items.

"What are you thinking babe?" Kyra was as intrigued as the rest of us.

"Let's wait for Trina then I'll explain." She was back in minutes. She ran back with the supplies and out of breath, asked Akylas his plan. He took a piece of paper and tore it to make a smaller piece.

"Everyone, write this down on pieces of paper about this size." He wrote...

> *Keep brain walls up while reading...mole inside...new plan...show up at designated time bags in hand...your bird will take you to other side of island...wait there til you are retrieved...DO NOT act suspicious..destroy this note by swallowing*

"Cool...this is a great idea!" Nikias grabbed paper and pen and began writing. The rest of us followed suit until we had 150 notes.

We all took regions and quietly woke everyone up and handed them their notes, with our fingers on our lips so they wouldn't speak out loud or in their minds. When the task was done we all backed to the middle of their sleeping grounds and looked at everyone. Each and every person nodded their heads that they understood.

I decided to test a few of them randomly and they passed with flying colors. Everyone's defenses were armed and ready. Again, we all went back to bed and tried to grab a couple hours' sleep. Never mind, no sleep for us. I think all of us lay there wide awake.

At exactly 5:45 a.m. I shot out of bed and poked Damien's foot. He had been resting his eyes, but he too did not sleep. He jumped up and we all met downstairs. Adam was sitting at the dining room table drinking a cup of coffee.

"Good morning all. Did you sleep well? I hope so 'cause we have a war to win and we need you rested." It didn't seem like he suspected so we played along. But what a crock!

"Yep we're rested and ready to kick some ass!" I decided that would be a safe thing to say considering it was completely true.

We gathered at the field with everyone and said our phony good-byes. I tested randomly again, with a big passing score on those I tried infiltrating. I loved this military talk, it was fun. Even though I was a civilian cop I always wished I'd joined the military and been an MP.

So far the plan was flawless. Everyone did exactly what was expected and Adam did not suspect a thing. By 4:00 p.m. everyone was on the other side of the island waiting for further instructions. Adam's bird returned to take him, supposedly, back to school. We had decided that Nikias would jump in his head and follow him. Zander would stay with Sebastian.

Trina and Adam hugged each other and he climbed on the back of his bird. We gave them about 30 minutes; then Trina gathered all remaining birds and instructed them to bring everyone back. Nikias and Zander stayed in the house concentrating on minds of their designated targets.

The birds brought all 150 'soldiers' to the training field and Trina filled them in on the situation and new plan. Everyone agreed it was an awesome plan and felt it would be easy to take down these thugs.

Trina said, "I have to admit, I was wrong. Nikias wanted to have all of you here and I really didn't feel it was necessary for that many people to get involved. I don't like putting all of you in this kind of danger since we are fighting our own kind. All of you have surpassed my expectations and I'm happy Nikias convinced me that more was better. The odds of any of you getting killed are minimal. But do not underestimate these maniacs. Never, for an instant, put down your guard…mentally or physically. I'm sure they will have their own acid rifles but I'm hoping they won't bring them to the meeting in two days. As long as no information is leaked, they won't have any reason to think there is a threat. Stay sharp and safe.

Now, go have some fun and then get lots of rest." Trina thanked everyone, then returned to the house to check on Nikias and Zander.

I followed her inside and we took a seat in the living room. We didn't want to disturb their concentration in the den. Trina turned on the television and we became couch potatoes for awhile.

Nikias strolled in first and seemed very pleased with himself, as usual.

"The little troll did just what he was supposed to. The bird dropped him in an alley in Las Vegas, Nevada. He met up with some grunt who took the fake papers, which by the way we didn't even have to change but whatever, and the grunt delivered them right to Sebastian. I had jumped into the grunt's head to see the exact location and I was right. I know exactly where this monster hides and the meeting is still scheduled. The grunt is gathering all the other grunts so they can meet day after tomorrow. I found Adam again and he returned to school like a good little boy." Nikias had such a way with words but I was happy to hear all was well. Now we needed an update from Zander about Sebastian. I remembered something that Nikias hadn't clued me in on yet.

"Hey, you never told me who the guy was that delivered the food to the snake."

"Just some idiot I graduated with. I hadn't seen him since and it threw me to know someone in my own class was a traitor. He wasn't the brightest bulb in the room. He let his guard down long enough for me to see their exact location and his thoughts took me right to their army. He was going over everything in his head and revealed the whole thing!" Nikias started laughing but stopped when he remembered Zander still needed quiet time.

Zander came into the living room about 30 minutes after Nikias with more good news. Not much to report but as far as he could tell, the meeting was still a go and no one suspected. Nikias, Zander and Trina went back to the party and I told them I would join them in a little while.

There was something gnawing at me and I wanted to make sure we weren't the ones being set up. I decided to get back into Adam's head while he was asleep. The school was eight hours ahead of us so Adam should be in a deep sleep by now. It was 8 p.m. our time so I snuck back to our room and concentrated on Adam's face. It didn't take long to get inside his brain.

> *I stayed on the sidelines, which was easy as he was talking to Sebastian inside the cave. I stayed outside the cave and was able to hear everything. Adam was really bad at sleeping with defenses, which was good for us.*
>
> *"Everything is going as planned Sir."*
>
> *"Good. We will all meet here tomorrow at 1:00 and assign everyone their region. We will take down the whole army. Once the strike begins, you bring Trina to me. I will have revenge for my brother's murder - then you will transform me and I will join the fight."*
>
> *"Sir, remember the transformation is not always successful with civilians, you could die."*
>
> *"That is a chance I will take. What do I have to lose? If I'm caught I go back to prison for the rest of my life. If the change is successful they will never be able to catch me." Adam nodded at him then left. I jumped out of his head before he spotted me.*

Well, unless that was a ruse, they don't suspect a thing. I still wanted us to stay sharp and not get cocky imagining this would be a breeze because of our numbers.

I ran outside and told Trina my concerns and she agreed. We gathered the whole clan again in the field; Trina and I stood on top of the bleachers so everyone could hear.

"Jesse has some valid concerns and it's always better to be safe than sorry. I've decided that we will go on with the plan but Jesse, Nikias, Zander, Damien, Akylas and Kyra will go out a few hours ahead. They will assess the situation and report back to me. If all is well then the rest of us will follow. It's a good thing our birds can get us places instantaneously. You will arrive in the area, quietly, at 11 a.m. and get into positions and after the little meeting has begun... you strike. Sebastian is the first target, then the rest.

Remember, there can be no sympathy for any of these traitors. If you recognize any of them don't hesitate, it's kill or be killed. They will be strategizing on our deaths and have already killed many of our future members, keep that in mind. Use that information to keep fury in your souls, you will need it for this battle. If your head starts to pound, push it out. Don't let any of them distract you with visions. They have the same powers and abilities that we do so keep your guard strong." Everyone clapped at the pep talk and seemed pumped.

"Trina, are you going to meet us out there?"

"No, Jesse I won't. I have to deal with a long-time friend and put him out of his and our misery." I knew she was speaking of Adam. I sensed a couple days ago that there had once been something between them, so I knew this really hurt her.

"I will position myself at the school early and write Abraams a note to fill him in. I haven't been able to tell him for fear of Adam or any of them overhearing. When you give me the okay, I will strike. We need to do this simultaneously so no warning can be given by any of them." Her face was filled with despair and I sincerely felt genuinely sorry for her.

The next morning we all ate breakfast, then every one of us got his/her rifle ready for travel. We checked and double checked that the weapons were in good working condition. There was tension in the air, you could have cut it with a knife. Most of us stayed quiet all day and remained deep in our own thoughts. We still had our walls up in protective mode, but the mood was heavy.

Nevada was 6 hours behind us but the six of us were leaving soon and getting hotel rooms outside of Vegas for tonight. We wanted to be close for tomorrow. We got our small duffel bags ready and put them by the front door. All six of us and Trina hung out in the house talking and trying to lighten the mood. Even Nikias was being nice with no sarcasm. We hugged Trina and told her to be careful, then grabbed our bags and headed to the field to "catch our bird". What an expression!

I said to those who weren't leaving yet, "Okay everyone. We'll see you in the morning. Stay safe and keep up your guards." They all waved good-bye as we climbed on Buzzard. I never thought I'd appreciate this old bird, but he was growing on me...everything about this new life and family was growing on me.

Chapter 7

War!

I had booked us at a hotel in Henderson, Nevada close to I-15. We would head down I-15 south in the morning.

Buzzard hovered over our hotel area until the coast was clear. Some people in a red car were retrieving their luggage out of the trunk in front of the hotel. The rest of the lot was clear, so Buzzard waited for them to leave and then brought us down at the side of the building. We all remained invisible until Buzzard was gone then walked around to the front. No one was out there so we returned to normal view, each holding our duffel bag, and walked through the front door.

I checked us in and the clerk gave us two keys to our rooms. Nikias, Damien and I would stay in one room, with Akylas, Kyra and Zander in the other. While we waited for the other three to settle in their room and meet us at ours, we decided to start strategizing. I put my bag on the floor next to one of the beds and couldn't move.

"Jesse, what's up?" Damien had sat on the other bed and was unzipping his duffel bag.

"I don't know. I can't shake this bad feeling. I'm sure everything is fine and the plan will go without a hitch, but there's something I can't put my finger on." That feeling had been nagging at me since yesterday when I went into Adam's head and heard their conversation. It sounded legit but still, that feeling would not go away.

"Jess, it will be okay."

"You're right. Let's get to work." The others showed up and we decided to grab some lunch downstairs before putting our heads together.

The rest of the afternoon was spent 'speaking' to Trina and figuring out the best positioning for our attack. Trina had arrived at the school shortly after we arrived in Nevada. She decided to stick close to Adam and feed him more false information. At some point she had excused herself, telling Adam she needed to use the restroom. She walked by Abraams office and slipped him the note she had written. Abraams read it with defenses up, then looked up at her and gave her the 'ok' sign, disappointment and disgust on his face. We tuned out with Trina and continued talking a few more minutes amongst ourselves.

After the 'pow-wow' some of them hung out at the pool and others stayed in and watched TV. I lay on the bed and got lost in defensive thought. I found Sebastian - nothing new with him - then found Adam, who had fallen asleep. I seized the opportunity and jumped into his head one more time. His wall was up. Was he not in a deep sleep yet? Was he suspicious and figured out how to sleep defensively?

Well, not going to worry about it. Sleep sounds good and everything will be fine tomorrow.

"*That's right little brother. You worry way too much. Get some rest and we will kick some ass tomorrow. Oh, and put your wall up, Nimrod.*"

"*Stay out of my head, Jerk.*" I put up my red brick wall and got comfortable in bed.

Damien had been watching television and turned it off when he saw Nikias and I settling in. The hotel had brought us a cot so Nikias slept on that. I was surprised he didn't argue about getting one of the beds but he made a cocky remark about Damien and I needing better sleep since we were the weaker ones. I knew then that all was normal.

I ignored him and got under the comforter. I decided to 'find' Mandy before falling asleep and make sure she was safe. I really wanted to get into her head and make her remember us but Nikias was right, oh how I hated admitting that, but she was safer not remembering.

I lay in bed with eyes closed and concentrated on her face. I would enter her head with my walls up so she wouldn't 'hear' or 'see' me.

Flashing images went through my head but they were of the past, things that had already happened. I can usually 'find' her right away in the present. I concentrated harder. I pictured the inside of the house trying to figure out what she may be doing now. There was nothing, no Mandy or even Sam. I pictured the outside and saw the barn and arena. I went back into the house and upstairs to her room, then Sam's…nothing, just an empty house. Maybe she and Sam went out to eat or to a movie…or both. But why can't I 'see' them?

Get a grip, I'm sure they're fine.

I cleared my head and just let my thoughts drift…

It started the usual way with Mandy and I together at the ranch. I was standing at the stove making bacon and eggs. Sam walked into the kitchen and sat down at the table with Mandy. I looked over my shoulder at the two of them. I thought of how wonderful a normal happy life was going be with them. Mandy pushed herself from the table and walked over and gave me a hug from behind. I put the spatula on the stove and turned to her. Then the strangest thing happened, I bent down to kiss her stomach…she was pregnant! I talked to my unborn child and patted her stomach then gave her a gentle but firm hug.

The next scene of the dream was the three of us sitting at the table eating, and then Mandy stood up.

"Ok, I have a class starting soon. I'll see you tonight after work. Sam, your bus will be here soon so get ready for school."

"*Ok Mandy and Jess, see ya tonight.*"

"*Alright, both of you be careful and I love you guys.*" Sam turned and walked out front for the bus and Mandy walked out back and blew me a kiss.

Suddenly I was in a police car in uniform. Awesome, I must have gotten a job with the local police department. I drove down a street, I assumed in Bozeman. It was a residential area with tidy lawns and big pine trees lining both sides of the street. A few people were outside mowing. I watched the typical suburban activity: a kid playing basketball; a girl riding her bike on the sidewalk; an older gentleman walking his dog on the other side of street, waving at me. It felt like a peek into the – hopefully - near future.

The peaceful scenes continued a little while longer. I drove up and down streets and just as I made a turn onto another street, it got dark as if someone had turned off the sun. I stopped the car in the middle of the street and sat there. I looked out the windshield, but then the car disappeared and I was standing in a dark forest! While still in my dream I turned to make sure my wall was up and sturdy, it was. I stood there for what seemed like hours, which happens in dreams. I stared into the darkness, barely able to see shadows of the trees. I looked up to the sky and caught mere glimpses through the thick trees.

I kept staring, wondering what was happening...it didn't take long to find out. Sebastian's face came charging at me - not his body, just his evil oblong disgusting face, floating in the air! It came within inches of me and stopped. He looked at me with no emotion for a few seconds, then broke into an evil laugh that sent chills up my spine. I stood frozen, saying and doing nothing. I reached out to hit him but he was gone. I looked all around me and saw my wall. It was up, no cracks or broken areas. How did he get in, or was it just a real nightmare? It had to be the latter!

I turned back toward where his face had been - still darkness until...Mandy! Her face came out of nowhere and stopped as Sebastian's had, but she was screaming and crying at the same *time - then a white cloth was clamped over her mouth. Just as she closed her eyes, she let out a "Jes..." Then in a swirling cloud, her face vanished!*

"MANDY! MANDY!" I screamed her name...

"MANDY!" I opened my eyes and realized I screamed that one out loud. I was sitting up and had been gripping the comforter so tight that it was in a sweaty ball around me. My fingers ached from clenching them into fists while clutching the covers and sweat ran down my face and into my eyes.

"What the hell is going on?! I was having a really good dream you jerk!" Nikias sat up and glared at me.

Damien was wide awake now too. "You okay Jesse?"

"Something is wrong. We're being set up!" I was trembling so violently, I could barely get the words out.

"You're such a drama king! We're not being set up, you said yourself that Adam knows nothing."

"I'm telling you, we're being set up. The worst part is, I think they have Mandy!"

"What?! Jesse are you sure?" That had Damien sitting up in his bed.

"I tried 'finding' Mandy before I went to sleep but no one was around, I couldn't find her anywhere, so I decided it was fine and went to sleep. I just had a nightmare about Sebastian and Mandy. I had my walls up so I'm not sure how he or Mandy got in, but they did, and she was screaming. Then a white cloth went over her mouth and she was gone. But she screamed a part of my name before she disappeared. I know she is in trouble and I'm sure Sebastian and his goons have her."

"The way to explain it is...a nightmare! That's all it was. Now go back to sleep, we have to get up in a few hours and you two need all the beauty sleep you can get." Nikias lay back down and turned away from us.

"Damien, I'm telling you, it's a setup. They have Mandy..." Then it occurred to me – Trina! She would be in danger as well.

"Jesse, what? What are you thinking?" Damien was sitting on the edge of his bed facing me.

"Hold on." I pictured Trina's face and she answered me immediately. I let her inside my wall along with Nikias and Damien...

"Jesse, what's up?"

"We have to abort! You need to get out of there, NOW!"

"What?! Why? What's going on?"

"I don't have time to explain, I just know we're being set up and Adam knows everything. I'm sure he has told Sebastian. I also think they have Mandy! Trina, get out of there and get to Nevada. We will re-group and figure out a new plan."

Nikias was furious. *"Mom, he's nuts! He had a nightmare and is convinced it was real. Everything is fine and we're going to stick with the original plan. Drama King, go to sleep!"*

"No, I think he's right." Damien piped in quietly. I looked at him and he was pacing between the beds, holding his head in his hands.

"Damien, did you see Cassie?" I thought he had just gotten a feeling about Cassie. If she got kidnapped again...I didn't want to think about it.

"No, but I think it's all my fault!"

"Wait, what? Damien, what's going on?" Trina's voice cracked with worry.

"Oh, that's just frigging great! Genius boy over here let Adam in! I was able to get in just now and saw it all! Adam knew the weakest link and slipped into Damien's head! We're all screwed, even your precious Mandy, Jesse!" Nikias was up by this point sitting on the edge of his cot, his eyes crimson.

"Nikias, calm down! Damien, tell us what happened. How do you know Adam got in?" Trina asked. She was trying to stay calm herself.

"The night Adam got to the island. I was sitting on the porch thinking about Cassie and the plan. I don't know where Adam was but

he must have sensed my defenses were down, I didn't even know they were down. But for a split second I saw his face in my head and then it was gone. I put up thicker walls right after that and concentrated on keeping them up. I never saw him in my head after that night so I thought everything was ok." He looked at me, his eyes pleading. *"Jesse, you said it looked like they didn't know a thing."*

"Well, I was wrong. They had to pretend not to know anything to get us right where they want us - here. Trina, now I don't think you should come here. Go back to the island and stay put. We will have all the others and outnumber them by - well, a lot. The others will be here in a few hours. I just need to find out for sure if they have Mandy. If they do we will have to get her out of there before anything else."

"No way! I'm not leaving my boys to fight my battle for me. I'm the one he is after and it's because of me that all those innocent people died. I will not sit by and let others fight this battle. I'm going to take care of Adam quickly so he doesn't have a chance to get a 'help' message to that S.O.B. then I'm on my way to Nevada. Don't do anything until I get there, I mean it...NOTHING!"

"Fine, but I don't like the idea." She tuned out and the three of us sat there for a minute staring at each other.

"I'm sorry. This is all my fault!" Damien sat down on his bed and hung his head, his shoulders sagging.

"Damn straight, it's your fault! In fact, I think you should go back to the island and try to keep your thoughts to yourself until this is over." Nikias fumed.

"Nikias, shut up! You're not helping the situation. It happened and there's nothing we can do about it now." Then I jumped into Damien's head, his wall was up. "Damien, did you have your defense up during this whole conversation?"

"Yes, I'm not going to make that mistake again." He looked at Nikias who was still glaring at him.

"Yeah, I haven't been able to get into his brain again. You better keep it up because if I find it down again, I'm gonna tear into you!"

I sat on my bed and thought for a second.

"Okay, they took Mandy because they know we have the numbers. They know we won't strike if there's an innocent civilian inside." My thoughts were racing, and I began to realize that Sebastian was probably holding her inside the cave! If he hurts her in any way…I will personally torture him and then kill him.

"It's obvious that he has been planning this for a long time and our idiot traitors must have helped him escape from prison. He knew that these killings would get our attention and eventually get to Mom. She is the key, but we have to keep her safe." Nikias had his thinking cap on and the wheels were turning, but he was stating the obvious.

"Okay, so what's our next move?" I asked Nikias. I looked at Damien, who was sitting on his bed, obviously torturing himself about what had happened.

"Damien, snap out of it and help us with the new plan. I know you feel bad but what's done is done." I couldn't continue to hold his hand and try making him feel better, we needed to figure this out quickly.

"Fine but I don't know what to do."

We all sat there in silence for a few minutes when I felt Trina's presence.

"Trina's here, you guys jump in." I opened my wall long enough for the three of them to get inside. Anytime we would converse inside my head I had images of the training field at the island, but this time I wanted Mandy's place to be the setting.

"Whoa, where are we little brother?" Nikias asked as he spun around looking at the scenery. Damien glared at him.

"What? Can't a guy ask a question?"

I said, *"Don't worry about where we are. Trina, what happened?"*

"It's done. Adam is taken care of and Abraams is on board with whatever we decide. He had an idea but Jesse, it's dangerous for Mandy."

"Let me hear it and I'll decide if we're going to do it."

"First, I told the others to stand by on the island until we give them the 'okay'. Second, Abraams' plan will work but it may get Mandy killed. We need to regain the element of surprise. Sebastian does not know that Adam is dead so we use that. Abraams will be able to imitate Adam's voice and 'talk' to Sebastian without showing himself, giving him false information. He will tell Sebastian that he is in hiding because we are on to him..." I had to interrupt her because I just had a thought.

"Sorry Trina but something just occurred to me. I couldn't 'find' Mandy before because they probably have her sedated so she would be in a comatose state. I tried finding Sam as well, but I really don't have a clear image of her.

If I concentrate harder I can get into Mandy's head quietly and see if I can find out more information. It also occurred to me that she must remember me because she yelled out part of my name when they grabbed her. I'll get in with my walls up and tell her not to say anything. Let me try - then we can go from there."

"Okay, we'll wait but hurry."

I closed my mind's eyes and concentrated...

> *I was in. I stood in total darkness for a minute or so. Then there was a crackling noise and the darkness gave way to the forest again. I was getting to know that place really well. I only had to walk a few steps before I stepped out of the forest and into the clearing by the lake, Mandy's lake. There she was, a vision of beauty and serenity sitting by a fire. I assumed that was the crackling noise. I watched her sitting there on a fallen log, staring at the flames. I crept a little closer keeping my defenses strong. She couldn't see or hear me. I needed to know if her images would turn to something I could use. I needed her to think about her true surroundings.*
>
> *I waited a few more minutes and almost gave up, when suddenly the serenity turned to violence. Darkness surrounded me again and she started breathing hard. I*

couldn't see her but heard the breathing. She then started mumbling and I couldn't make it out at first...but when I understood, I almost phased right there in her head. She was coming out of her sedation and that troll was talking to her. I tried to remain calm and stood in the dark listening.

"Hello sleepy head. Don't worry, I'm not going to put you to sleep again. I want your boyfriend to 'hear' and 'see' you so he understands he'd better do what I say. Jesse, if you're listening, here are my demands. Keep your army away and bring me Trina, only you. If my guys find that anyone else is with you, this beautiful young thing dies. I want Trina here tonight at six sharp." I jumped into his demented head so I could 'see' Mandy's condition. He had no idea but it was difficult to remain calm and quiet when I saw her and heard what he said.

She was lying on a filthy cot on the other side of the cave and her hands were tied behind her back. There was a black bandana covering her eyes and duct tape on her mouth. Tears were rolling down her cheeks and she moaned and squirmed a little. I wanted desperately to jump out of his head, rip him into pieces then grab Mandy and never let her go.

"Aw, gotta quit that moving and get comfortable. You're not going anywhere until I see Trina. Oh and Jesse...if you are here, I have sixteen of my men situated throughout the country and at the top of every hour until six tonight, one more of your kind will die. Well, the ones that aren't changed yet, you know, still civilians. They are so much easier to kill that way. I sure hope you're listening, Jesse." Then, that revolting, evil troll put his hand on Mandy's cheek! I nearly lost it. I knew if I didn't get out of there and back to reality I would get Mandy killed, as I would end up revealing I was there and say something stupid.

I jumped back into my head and joined the other three still inside my wall. They had been anxiously waiting for me to return. I couldn't catch my breath in my head or body.

"Well, he must have 'seen' her but he looks pretty pissed off." Nikias grinned at me and I almost jumped out of my head and tore him up for real.

"Nikias, knock it off! What happened, Jesse?" Trina had a tranquil voice even when she was angry. It calmed me enough to tell them what happened and what the troll said.

Trina said, "That does it! It's two a.m. now, so that gives us sixteen hours to come up with a new plan. We need to start from scratch but can't take the chance on any of them finding or hearing us. I want all of you to return to the island now. The birds are on their way to pick you up. I'll meet you there." She tuned out and Damien and Nikias jumped out of my head.

"Damien, keep your walls up until this whole thing is over." I knew he knew that but I really needed to reiterate the point. It was more crucial now than ever.

We returned to the island and everyone regrouped in the training field. Trina and Nicos stood at the podium. She reminded everyone to keep their guards up while we formulated a new plan. We couldn't take the chance on any of them figuring out what we were up to, again.

Trina told them everything that happened. For the next hour all of us, including most of the 150 soldiers, threw out ideas. One person would make a suggestion, while twenty others would argue why that wasn't a good idea and so on. I knew everyone had good intentions and it wasn't just Mandy and Trina we're trying to keep safe, it was our family's entire future. But the clock was ticking, literally. Every minute that passed was another minute that maniac had his hands on Mandy. I couldn't stand it any longer. I touched

Trina on the shoulder and motioned her to step aside. I got in front of the mic to speak to everyone.

"I just want you to know how we all appreciate everyone's support and we will figure this out..." In that second, it hit me! I knew what we had to do and it would keep everyone safe!

"Everyone please sit tight. We will be right back." I stepped away from the podium and grabbed Trina by the arm.

"Jesse, what is it?" All six of them gathered around me in anticipation.

"Okay. I tell Sebastian that Trina and I will be there at six p.m. but he is to get his army back and not to kill anyone else." I walked over to a tree branch and picked it up. I made a picture of Sebastian's hideout in the dirt.

"His goons will be protecting him from the outside, probably scattered at all angles so they can see or hear anyone who approaches. He might have a couple inside the cave. If he doesn't agree to bring in the sixteen we'll deal with that. Unfortunately, a few more civilians may die, but I hope not. He probably has killed at least one more since it's been over an hour.

Trina, is there any way we can get the acid in something and drop like fire retardant? Buzzard and the other birds can carry the container and drop it on his army." I took a breath and looked up at all of them staring at me.

"I'm sure we can figure something out. Oh, the same type of metal our rifles are made of." I could tell she saw where I was going with this plan as there was a lot of enthusiasm in her voice.

"Jesse, this will work! By the time the acid starts to fall it will be too late for them! The birds and containers will be invisible. We kill them all in one swoop!" I had never heard Trina talk like that, it was awesome! Then she continued.

"Jesse...you, Nikias, Zander and Akylas will storm in and take Mandy. When you have her out, I will deal with Sebastian. Then we will deal with the remaining sixteen if they don't return."

"He might have one or two in the cave with him so we need to be invisible and armed when we go inside, to take them out as well." We all agreed this was an excellent plan and turned to the people in the field to help us figure out the details, the largest being how to devise a system for the birds to hold and drop the acid like fire retardant.

"Wait a minute, we haven't figured out the containers that will hold the acid. That is probably the most important detail of this plan, right?" Damien blurted out.

Trina looked at Nicos who nodded his head.

"Yes Damien, that is a very important detail and one that is already taken care of." Nicos looked to Trina to finish the explanation.

"The school has a basement below the basement with all the supplies and ammunition we need. In our history we've never had to use the kettles, the containers, as that is reserved for mass killings of enemies. We have trained Buzzard and the other Ahools on the use of these kettles in the event of a war on our own kind. They are all on their way to school as we speak to collect them and should be back any time."

Damien looked at me for reassurance. He was hoping I had confidence in this complicated plan.

"It'll work Damien." I didn't want to say anything else as I was a little nervous about this plan myself.

"Okay, time for bed. We have probably the most important day of our existence tomorrow."

By four a.m. we were ready go to. We were flown by the birds in stages to the nearest destination possible without being detected. Buzzard and his crew would then return to retrieve the kettles which would be filled with the acid. The kettles all had secure lids made of the same material so none would be lost on the journey. When all the Ahools returned, we would take off the lids and prepare for battle. Those of us on the ground were armed with acid rifles.

By seven a.m., everyone was in place. We all kept our defenses solid.

We all brought duffel bags with food and water. Many decided to take a quick nap while they waited for the action to begin. Trina, standing about 50 yards from the napping soldiers, motioned for the six of us and Nicos.

"Jesse, go ahead and tell Sebastian that we will be there at six. Let's get this plan in motion and get Mandy out of there. I just 'spoke' to Abraams and he's been busy pretending to be Adam. He said Sebastian is convinced Adam is alive and well but in hiding."

"Sounds good to me. Hang tight while I make a deal with the devil." I walked to a boulder that sat near the lake and rested against it. I closed my eyes and pictured the troll.

"Sebastian, it's Jesse. Trina and I will be there at six tonight - but you need to have the rest of your army return here and don't hurt any more civilians. I also want proof of life." My skin crawled at the thought of her being with that psycho.

"Aw, hi Jesse. It's nice to finally meet you. It was a lucky break that your poor unsuspecting brother, Damien, let one of my loyal comrades invade his brain. If not for your brother, you would have the upper hand and I never would have known of this beautiful creature." I had only been 'speaking' to him but then I jumped into his head and made my presence known. I just needed to make sure Mandy was okay.

"Oh now I can see you. Hard to believe you're my nephews! Family reunions are usually emotional, but hmmm...I feel nothing. It's tough to feel the love when my brother was killed because of you four. But Trina will be the only casualty. I just cannot justify taking the lives of my nephews unless you force my hand.

You understand why I need justice?" He was such an obnoxious cretin that I couldn't wait for Trina to get her hands, or claws, whichever way she chose, around his scrawny neck. I kept checking my mind's walls as I pictured destroying this cock roach. I looked through his evil eyes as he stared straight ahead at the cave wall. He knew I was 'watching' and didn't want to give too much information.

I played along. "Oh sure, I understand. But I don't understand how our mother could fall for such a mutant family! You and Petros disgust me. But I digress. Pull your men back."

"I'll think about bringing my men back but not making any promises – or, I might have them continue their killing spree until tonight. I haven't decided yet."

"You bastard. How many have you killed since this morning?"

"Hey now, no need for name calling. Three. I told you one an hour, the number dead should be five but I was feeling generous."

"Before I leave, I want to see Mandy." He closed his eyes while he turned his head, which told me he had at least one guard in there with him. He opened them and there she was! Still tied and gagged and from the looks of it, sedated again.

"I'll see you at six to see you burn in hell with your brother! I'm sure he's missing you down there!" I jumped out of his head before he could have the last word.

"It's done. They think they have until six tonight but we got the element of surprise back on our side! Let's get these monsters and get on with our lives!" I looked at Trina and she nodded her head.

So we quietly walked around and woke the soldiers up and moved closer to Sebastian's hideout. Buzzard had been sleeping by one of the cacti and Trina asked him to fly her over the target area to scope it out.

The air was hot and dry even this early in the morning. Desert heat is brutal, but the thought of seeing Mandy soon kept me cool and collected. Buzzard and Trina came back a few minutes later.

We then gathered to hear Trina's report.

"The situation looks good. Most of them are sleeping, some in jag form and some human. There are a few walking around but it's quiet. Buzzard will take me, Jesse, Nikias, Akylas and Zander to a spot just outside the area close to the cave where Sebastian is hiding. The rest of you will be placed strategically surrounding the entire area. No one will get past us!" Trina took a deep breath and looked around. When none of us asked any questions, she continued.

"There are 150 of us. The instant the birds drop the acid there will be chaos. Have your rifles ready and don't let anyone get through your mind's wall or physically push through. Remember, you will have to stay in human form to operate the HF rifles. Some of the traitors may have phase into jag form. Don't let that distract you, aim and fire. Keep your defenses up. Don't let any of them play mind games; if your head pounds, it's a vision, shake it off." She looked at me after that comment, then continued.

"Stay sharp and alert. I'm really hoping by the time you get to the location it will all be over and you can go home to your families. This fight is for them and all future Family members. Be safe out there." All responded with a head nod. The five of us climbed on Buzzard and took off.

Buzzard flew slow and invisible so we wouldn't disturb the sleeping enemy. He landed on a ridge located east of the cave. We jumped off and positioned ourselves. Buzzard immediately took off to help gather rest of the soldiers before grabbing his kettle.

The five of us had a perfect vantage point and could see everyone who slept or wandered outside. We lay on the ground behind some brush that bordered the ridge around the cave staying invisible and quiet.

I wanted to 'see' Mandy but forced myself to stay out of Sebastian's head. I couldn't take any chances. We had about forty-five minutes before the Ahools would arrive. I counted the guards outside – there were 39. Sebastian must have the other 3 goons in the cave with him.

I felt like we were in a war movie, crouched and waiting for the enemy to make a move. My HF rifle was loaded and ready. I kept it tucked under my right arm. The ground we were lying on was rocky and painful but we remained calm and cool. Trina kept in contact with the Ahools so they would know the exact second to grab their kettles.

She looked one more time at us and I gave her a nod. Trina closed her eyes and mentally told Buzzard it was a go. There was a faint roaring sound in the air from their massive wings. No one below stirred - they had no idea that sound meant their demise. All of us remained in position, but ready to pounce.

The sound got closer and the scene below us changed slowly. The goons who had been sleeping woke up, but didn't seem concerned. The ones who had been in jag form phased back and gathered clothes to put on. All of their eyes looked up toward the sky. It was as if they were all our puppets. They began to gather closer together so they could talk to each other. Perfect! My only concern was the troll in the cave. I worried he would step outside with Mandy. I prayed silently that he would not be suspicious and would stay in the cave with her.

Their voices carried up the ridge. We didn't have to read their minds as we heard the conversations. My heart began to hammer in my chest; my head started sweating and my hands were clammy.

"What is that noise?" One of the idiots asked.

"I don't know, there's nothing up there." Another idiot responded.

The birds were about one hundred yards out. Buzzard knew we were on the ridge. After dropping the acid they would veer away from the ridge. The sound now became deafening.

The goons gathered even closer together still looking to the sky.

I carefully thought to myself, *keep close together as you are making the birds' jobs so much easier.*

The birds were in position. On the handles of the kettles was a lever their talons could move which would tip the container upside down. The traitors were getting a little nervous but still didn't go out of formation. Instinct took over and they stayed close together in front of the cave to ward off danger.

All of them had HF rifles pointed in the air toward the humming noise. Then it happened! The Ahools dropped the Hydrofluoric Acid over the entire area and hit every one of them in one pass! The Ahools came out of hiding so the enemy could see their attackers. The goons held their heads and ran in every direction. In a few short minutes it was over. They had all lay on the ground screaming and writhing from the acid eating them alive. It was a horrific scene but we had to stay focused. It was our cue to move.

We heard stirrings in the cave and all defenses were down and panicking. The cave would hold Mandy, Sebastian and his only remaining guard. The other 2 guards had run down to the others just before the acid dropped. We had to play this carefully and quickly. The rest of our crew came running from all direction and circled the cave's entrance.

I motioned for the others sitting with me to jump in my head inside the wall…

"I'm going to talk to Sebastian from here. Nikias, Akylas and Zander go around on top of the cave's entrance. When he comes out, one of you hit the guard with acid, another jump on Sebastian and the third, grab Mandy. Trina you stay here. If he gets a hold of you somehow, it's all over." She nodded but didn't look happy about letting her sons do the fighting.

"Done." Nikias said as he grabbed the other two and they raced to their positions.

"Okay, Jesse, how do you want this to play out?" Sebastian yelled at me from inside the cave. Coward. I kept my walls up so his guard would not read our plans.

"You let Mandy out unharmed and we'll send in Trina." Trina was crouched next to me ready and anxious for the fight.

"You're a funny man. It will be the other way around. Send Trina to the mouth of the cave and when I see she is alone, I'll give you Mandy."

"We're on our way!" Trina yelled and started running down the ridge! Damn it, she is going to get herself and Mandy killed! I could feel the tension in Nikias building even though he was several hundred yards away. I had grown to care for Trina so having both my favorite ladies in the face of danger made my blood churn.

Trina reached the mouth of the cave and stayed a safe distance away so Nikias and the other two could see her.

"Sebastian, I'm here. Let Mandy walk out of there alone." It took a few minutes - which felt like hours for him to respond. I tried getting into his head and his guard's but they both had their walls up. Whoever taught that trick to Sebastian did a good job, unfortunately. I couldn't get a sense of their next move and it was driving me insane. The rest of our army still held their positions ready and armed. Some of them gathered behind Nikias and Akylas.

"All right, she is coming out but with my guard. He will let her go when you are in his grip."

"Fine. This is between you and me anyway. Let's get this over with."

"Patience. I want to savor this moment." I had no doubt he had something else up his sleeve but all I could do was wait and watch. The next couple of minutes were a blur and I'm still not sure what happened first.

The guard and Mandy appeared in the doorway. My entire body tensed. I didn't realize how hard I clenched my teeth until my jaw began to hurt. I looked at my hands and the palms were bloody from making fists.

Mandy's face was caked with dirt and tears. He kept her blindfolded and gagged but her hands were loose. The goon held on to her upper left arm.

The guard and Mandy took a couple more steps and Trina did the same. They were all within inches of each other. Suddenly, the guard grabbed Trina's arm and let Mandy go at the same time. His rifle was on a strap around his left shoulder. He pulled Trina to his right side and started to take his rifle off his shoulder. Just as he slung it down to his left hand, Trina wriggled away and grabbed it from him.

In the meantime, Mandy had pulled off her blindfold and was running, while ripping the tape off her mouth. I took my eyes off Trina for a second and screamed at Mandy!

"MANDY, UP HERE! RUN!" She stopped, turned and ran for the ridge.

I looked back at Trina and she had the rifle aimed at the guard. One of the Ahools they had brainwashed into being their transportation appeared out of nowhere. He had been told to swoop down invisibly and grab the three on top of the cave. Just as his talons touched the tip of Nikias' shoulder, Buzzard suddenly swooped in! They both turned visible and Buzzard hit the enemy bird so hard that it knocked him out momentarily. Buzzard swooped in and picked him up by the neck and torso piercing his heart. The enemy bird died instantly, Buzzard flung him off the battle field.

Nikias, Akylas and Zander jumped down on top of the guard and killed him quickly. The rest of our army moved in and surrounded the cave opening.

"JESSE, STAY WITH MANDY!" Trina had yelled from the ground. No problem there. I held her tight on the ground under my arm. Everything happened so quickly that I couldn't even enjoy the feeling of having the love of my life in my arms once again.

I watched the scene below intently for signs of trouble or the need for my help. The worst was over, now it was a game of cat and mouse with Sebastian. I knew Trina would enjoy this immensely.

Buzzard came back alone, a little tattered from the struggle but okay. He landed near us and Mandy almost came unglued. She struggled to get away from me so she could run from the creature. I had forgotten that he was a fearful sight to her. The enemy Ahool must have stayed out of her sight.

"Mandy, it's okay. He's our friend. He won't hurt you, I promise." I couldn't help but chuckle. She looked at me with those beautiful ginger eyes but very serious and cute.

"Really? A huge creature almost crushes us and you're laughing?!"

"Yes, really. It's okay, he won't hurt you. You can even pet him."

"Um, no!" We turned our gaze back to the scene below. I did catch Mandy looking behind us at Buzzard a few times. He would just cock his head and stare at her, probably laughing in his own birdlike way.

Trina finally called out. "C'mon Sebastian. You know you're surrounded and have lost this war. There is no way out." Silence. Everyone started looking around at each other but didn't move until Trina gave the okay. She held her ground a few more minutes.

Just as she and the others took a step toward the cave opening, all hell broke loose again! Buzzard suddenly fell to the ground, with dust and dirt flying everywhere! I had no idea what happened until I felt Mandy being ripped from my arms by Sebastian! He had his slimy paws on her again!

"Thought you had me didn't you? The cave has a tunnel that goes right under your feet and the opening is over there." He gestured behind him with his head and his left arm around Mandy's neck. He held an acid rifle in the right. I wasn't sure at that moment how he took down Buzzard but I had to focus on Mandy.

"Now, we're going to do this again - but the right way and my way this time. Send that Trina bitch up here NOW!" Sebastian couldn't see the cave opening from his stance and my back had been to it since he had grabbed Mandy. I slowly turned around to find Trina. None of them were in their original positions. Everyone was gone! I knew they must have circled around. I also figured they had all gone invisible.

"Hey cock roach! Behind you!" Trina, Nikias, Akylas and Zander appeared out of thin air ten feet behind him and Mandy.

Sebastian turned slightly to his right and bent his head around to see Trina. As he turned to face Trina, I phased and dived into his left side with my head cocked sideways. Before my teeth dug into his side below his ribs I gently knocked Mandy out of the way with my head. I caught the terror in her eyes but couldn't lose focus.

She fell to the ground but quickly scrambled to her feet. Zander scooped her up and brought her to safety.

My teeth tore into Sebastian but just as I was going in for the kill...

"MOVE JESSE, HE'S MINE!"

I released immediately - Trina had phased and came in on the other side. Sebastian screamed in agony but Trina didn't let him suffer very long. In seconds his lifeless body lay on the ground. It was over. There was complete silence except for normal desert sounds and a slight breeze in the air.

Trina and I phased to human form at the same time and for a fraction of a second, I had forgotten that Mandy was on the sidelines watching in terror and staring at me with no clothes on! It took that billionth of a second for two of our soldiers to grab extra clothes from their duffel bags and give them to Trina and me. We got dressed, looked at each other, then yelled at the top of our lungs...

"THE WICKED WARLOCK IS DEAD!" We had read each other's thoughts and decided to say that at the same time. Everyone dropped their guns and the tension left the air. All the guys and gals high fived and chest bumped each other. Shrieks of joy filled the desert morning air! A few of our people gathered around and picked up me, Nikias and Trina on their shoulders and walked us around singing, "For they are jolly good fellows..."

After they set us down, reality immediately set in. Buzzard and Mandy. I ran to Mandy, who was sitting on the ground paralyzed with fear. Trina and Nikias ran to Buzzard.

"He's coming around. That troll shot a tranquilizer into him! He's okay though!" Nikias yelled.

I ran a few feet toward Mandy then saw how terrified she was. Her face was blank, she didn't blink for a long time. I stopped a foot in front of her and knelt down on my knees to face her.

"Mandy...honey, it's over. It's really over this time, there are no bad guys left in this war." I reached out to put my hand on her shoulder and she jumped up and backed away from me.

"Over?! What the hell just happened?! Who are all these people...who are you?" She stood staring at me for a minute with no recognition in her eyes. She glanced at Buzzard, who was getting back to his feet. Damien and Kyra had gotten to the field shortly after the battle began and stood by Nikias. Mandy turned her gaze to Trina, Nikias, Akylas, Kyra; then back to Nikias and Damien who were standing side by side. She stared at the two of them intently then looked at me. I knew what she was wondering without reading her mind.

All of our people stood frozen, no one moved or said a word. Tension had returned, but it was empathy tension for Mandy.

"Mandy, I can explain." I broke the silence while she stared a hole into me.

"Explain which part?! Where are we? Who was that monster? Who are all these people? How did you turn into that...that.." She grabbed her stomach and ran away from all of us. I got up and started to run to her but Trina stopped me.

"Jesse, let her go. She needs to process everything that has happened. She will be okay, there is nowhere for her to run." Trina had walked up behind me when she could tell this wasn't going well and put her hand on my shoulder as I got up. I knew she was right, but it felt wrong.

I watched Mandy run, holding her stomach the entire time. She went behind a tree and I figured she was literally sick. The horror she must have felt watching all those people die, then seeing a man become a jaguar and tear into her captor.

I sat down on the hard ground and waited. Soft conversations began throughout the group, rehashing the victorious battle. Thirty minutes later, Mandy came walking back but stopped about fifty feet from all of us. She stood there staring at each and every one of us.

"Does anyone have any gum or breath mints?" Of all the words I expected out of that beautiful mouth, those words I did not see coming. A few of us chuckled, then Kyra walked over cautiously and gave her a piece of gum. Kyra took a step backward when Mandy took the gum from her hand; they stared at each other for a minute.

"Thank you."

"You're welcome. Um, are you okay? I know we must seem like a bunch of freaks but we're nice freaks, I promise." Mandy took a deep breath then looked at me. I took that cue and stood up. I cautiously stepped toward her. Kyra returned to Akylas who put his arm around her shoulder. Everyone was quiet again and waited for Mandy's next move.

"Jesse, is that your name? You need to explain all of this to me. When that monster took me from the barn, or whatever grabbed me, I had weird flashbacks or something. When I was grabbed, I saw your face...or his, or maybe his." She looked at me, Damien and Nikias. Mandy turned her attention back to me and stood another moment. Suddenly, her face went pale and she clutched her head falling to her knees! I started to run to her but she held out one of her arms. I stopped.

"Jesse, her memories are returning. Give her a few minutes." Trina said telepathically. Several miserable minutes went by and felt helpless and terrified at the same time. Then a miracle happened....

"Jesse, it's you! It's really you!" Mandy jumped up and ran into my arms. The relief I felt cannot be explained in words. I closed my eyes and held her.

She pulled back slightly but stayed in my embrace and looked at Damien and Nikias. Everyone stayed put and didn't move or say a word, just stared at Mandy.

"Thank you everyone for saving my life. Even you big ugly bird." Buzzard bowed his head in acknowledgement. She sat down on a boulder that was next to us and explained what had happened.

I could feel the rage come back as she spoke of the monster that held her captive. She and her sister, Cassie, always seemed to be in danger because of us. But could the danger finally be over? Would we finally be able to live happily ever after?

"Skittles, we gotta stop meeting like this!" I wanted to break the mood and see if I could put even a small smile on that gorgeous face. She stared at me stone-faced for a couple of seconds, then broke into a laugh which turned into more tears. I picked her up and hugged her like there was no tomorrow. She didn't push me away this time but instead, buried her face into my shoulder and hugged me tight. I held her and let her cry it out. She finally stepped backward, sniffing and looked up at me.

"Jesse, you sit down with her and explain our bizarre story while the rest of us clean up. We have some trash to take care of." Trina winked at me and motioned everyone to leave us alone.

An hour or so later we were ready to leave. Trina contacted all the birds and we agreed to go to the island to wash up, have a magnificent feast and then celebrate. It would be awhile before everyone was back on the island, the birds would bring them in shifts starting with us.

Buzzard knelt down for us to load and Mandy froze.

"It's okay. He is our ride to the island. He won't hurt you and I won't let anything happen to you, I promise. Mandy planted her feet, looked up at me and smiled...

"I've heard that before, Scooby." She unplanted her feet and let me help her aboard Buzzard's back.

Chapter 8

The Island Party

Everyone spent the next several days eating, drinking, dancing, phasing and swimming. Mandy and I would sneak away for hours at a time to catch up then a lot of kissing and cuddling. I couldn't remember the last time I felt this happy, oh wait, it was six months ago on a different island. The second night we decided to be a little more sociable.

"Jesse and Mandy, c'mon! We're gonna watch a movie. We have a projector and screen, it will be like a drive in without the cars!" Kyra yelled at us and everyone laughed. Mandy got up while holding my hand and gazed down at me. It was my turn to be paralyzed, not with fear but with sheer joy. I couldn't stop staring but that didn't stop her from tugging at my hand.

"That sounds fun, let's go." Mandy was stunning. The moment grabbed me. Even though I wasn't prepared, I didn't care. I kneeled on one knee and grabbed her hands in mine. She looked at me with questions in her eyes.

"Mandy?" Suddenly my voice cracked and my mouth went dry.

"Jesse, you're scaring me. Are you okay?" Could she be that naïve that she couldn't see what was coming next? That made me more nervous but I pushed through it.

"Marry me! Make me the happiest man on the planet!" Her hands went limp and her legs began to shake. I jumped up and grabbed her to keep her from falling. She regained her composure but now I wasn't sure if I wanted to hear the answer. Maybe whole ordeal had freaked her out too much. Did I ask way too soon? Did she still feel the same way as last year? These questions and more went racing and swirling in my head until…

"YES!!! I WILL MARRY YOU!!" Mandy jumped into my arms and wrapped her legs around my waist. She threw her arms around my neck crying and laughing at the same time. I hugged her tight and twirled around in a circle, almost falling down. We both laughed while I set her down then realized we had an audience. There was an eruption of cheering and clapping.

We all celebrated a while longer, then settled into the movie. Mandy and I sat on a blanket way in the back, behind the crowd. Nikias, Damien and Zander sat near us in lawn chairs. Kyra and Akylas were on the other side of us on their own blanket. Mandy sat between my legs and leaned against my chest. She had wrapped us in another blanket, as there was a chill in the night air. I noticed she had glanced at Damien and I knew the wheels were turning. I wanted to read her mind but didn't want to invade her privacy. I didn't need to, she sat up and whispered in my ear.

"We should surprise Damien and get Cassie out here." I had explained what Nikias had done to their memories and promised to restore everything back to normal. I would hold him to that.

"I'm a step ahead of you."

"Huh?"

"My secret." I had thought of that earlier today after getting to the island and pulled Nikias aside while Mandy was in the shower. I wanted to surprise Mandy and Damien.

Nikias agreed and fulfilled his promise. He restored Cassie and the families' memories. I then jumped into Cassie's head and explained everything that had happened in the last six months to us and her sister. When she stopped freaking out I told her Mandy and Damien were safe and sound. Cassie was so relieved.

"All of us have been frantically searching for Mandy! Tony and Becca had taken Sam into their home until Mandy was found. Jesse I can't tell you how happy I am!" Cassie agreed to contact everyone and give them the good news. Buzzard would pick her up in the morning. Everything was arranged. Damien would be thrilled.

The next morning I got up before Mandy and went downstairs for coffee. I noticed Damien sitting at the dining room table looking a little sad. I knew why but had to pretend I had no clue. It wouldn't be long before his sadness turned to joy.

I walked past him with my walls up so he wouldn't get a glimpse of his surprise and patted him on the shoulder. Then I walked past the living room toward the front door and noticed Nikias sitting in front of the TV. He had the remote in his hand and was watching a recorded news episode with that reporter I had seen in Mandy's house when I spied on her. He kept rewinding to a close-up of this lady as she was closing her segment.

"This is Sara Jackson signing off." Nikias stopped the recording with the reporter's smiling face taking up most of the screen and just stared at the screen.

I took my coffee outside on the front porch. Trina was already out there talking to a group of people who were getting ready to leave. They wanted to stay longer but needed to get back to their lives. Trina noticed me on the porch and joined me.

"What's with Nikias and the reporter lady?"

"Oh, Sara. All I know is that she was the love of his life. I'm not sure what happened, he won't talk about it. I do know that Akylas' brother, Zander, was with her first and somehow Nikias and Sara fell in love and I'm sure that's what drove a wedge between Nikias and Zander." Trina stopped with that story and changed the subject.

"I have something for you." She reached in her pocket and pulled out a little navy blue box and handed it to me. I opened the box and inside was the most gorgeous ring I had ever seen. It was beyond anything I would've picked out and the fact it was a family heirloom meant the world to me. The ring was a 14K two-tone white gold band with two rose gold settings. Nestled in the center of the roses were more diamonds. The ring was astonishing.

"It was your great-grandmother's and now it's yours to give to Mandy." I couldn't move. I looked at her and she had tears welling in her eyes.

"Trina, are you sure?"

"I'm positive. It is too beautiful to hide in a box." We stood up and hugged. Trina sat back down and grabbed my hand. We both sat in silence for a few moments.

"Hey you two, can I join or is this a private family conversation?" Mandy walked onto the porch.

"Honey, you are family." Trina stood and hugged Mandy. She headed down the stairs to continue saying her good-byes to the others.

"Mandy, give me her hand." She started to put her right hand in mine. I took her left and pulled the ring out of the box. I looked in those ginger eyes which were tearing up. I placed the ring on her finger, it fit perfectly.

"Jesse it is absolutely phenomenal! I love it!" She held her hand out in front of her face turning her wrist in half turns watching the sunlight bounce off.

We were brought back to earth by groups of people coming up to say good-bye as their time got closer to board their birds.

An hour later Nikias, Damien, Akylas, Kyra, Zander and Nicos all grabbed lawn chairs and sat on the front porch with us. Mandy had not taken her eyes off the ring and showed it off to all of them.

We watched as each Ahool loaded groups of people, spread their giant wings and fly off with their passengers. Before we knew it, everyone was gone.

The nine of us remained and sat quietly on the porch, drinking our coffee. We all knew of the upcoming surprise except Damien of course. Even Mandy kept up her walls once we taught her how to do it, she was a natural. Damien was the first to break the silence.

"Hey, Buzzard didn't come back. Shouldn't he have returned by now?" Damien's question could not have had better timing. None of us had to answer because seconds after the words came out of Damien's mouth, Buzzard came swooping down and landed in the training field. The sun was in our eyes but it was obvious he had a passenger.

Damien stood up and put his hand above his eyes to block out the sun.

"Did he forget to drop someone off? Wait a minute...is that... that's not Cas...!" Damien cut himself off and ran down the steps when he realized it was Cassie. It was just like a movie, they ran into each other's arms. Damien picked her up and swung her around like a rag doll.

We all stood up and clapped. Mandy stood up with us but couldn't stand it any longer. She ran down the steps and joined her sister and Damien. All three hugged each other and cried.

All of us stayed on the island for another week and spent time with Trina. We would sit around camp fires at night and she and Nicos would tell us stories of the past.

The days flew by until it was time for us all to start living a normal life. Trina explained that she would 'check' in with us once a month and we would be on call in case of an emergency. Other than those two commitments, we would be on our own to live as we chose. Of course we agreed to visit her on the island frequently.

Buzzard and two of his buddies were set to take us to our destinations. Damien and Cassie would take one; Akylas, Kyra and Zander would take the other and Mandy and I would fly with Buzzard. Nicos decided to stay awhile longer with Trina and Nikias.

"Well brothers, it's been...hmmm...a ride but it's time to say good-bye, for now. Don't worry, I'll keep your lives interesting." Nikias warned as he walked up to all of us. I motioned for him to walk off with me.

"Well little brother I guess this good-bye for now but I wanted to say something. You and I had a lot of moments to put it nicely and I don't know what's up with that gorgeous girl on TV but if she's the one, go get her." I fully expected him to smack me but he never stops surprising me.

"Already on it big bro." He put his arm around my neck and pulled me down to the ground. I jumped up and gave him a nod before heading back to Buzzard and the others.

We all hugged before loading onto Buzzard. Trina stood with Nicos tears streaming down her face. Nikias had his usual smirk on his face.

Buzzard took us to Montana; Damien and Cassie flew to Florida to spend time with the girls' parents. Akylas and Kyra were flown to Kyra's hometown in Idaho. We had exchanged phone numbers and swore we would all keep in touch - which we did, by the way.

Chapter 9

Home

Life slowly returned to normal in Montana. I called the police department in Boulder and they gave a recommendation to the department in Bozeman. A week later I was sworn in. I hired a moving company to pack and load my house in Boulder and deliver my things to Mandy's house.

Mandy, Sam and I settled in together and it seemed like my dream. While I waited for my start date at work, I would watch Mandy teach and help around the ranch as much as I could. Tony and Becca were very welcoming and helpful and some evenings we would barbecue with them.

Two days before I started work, Mandy and I decided to go for a ride. She saddled one of the gentler horses for me and we headed out on a trail. It was the same trail the bear chased us out of when I 'spying' on her. I had not told Mandy about the 'watchful eye' I had kept on her the last few months, I decided to keep my mouth shut awhile longer.

"I don't want to scare you but a couple months ago there was a black bear up here that chased me and Zamira down the trail to the barn. Animal Control got him and took him to the other side of the mountain." I acted surprised but of course, I already knew.

"Where are we going?" I knew that answer as well.

"My favorite place. I go there to decompress and think or not think of anything at all. The only other person I've brought here is Sam. You should feel very special." She laughed and kept riding ahead of me.

"Oh...I do."

The spot was more beautiful in real life than it was in her head. We dismounted and walked the horses to the edge of the lake to drink. We stood between the horses holding hands and looked at the water. The horses made a quiet sucking noise as they drank some water. When Zamira was done he held up his head, water dripping from his mouth. Mandy walked to the saddle bag on the back of her saddle and pulled out what she called grazing ropes. She unbridled both horses and hooked the ropes to their halters that had been on under the bridles.

We tied them to separate trees and found our own spot on some thick short grass under a big shade tree. I leaned against the tree and Mandy sat between my legs and against my chest, again. That was becoming a very comfortable position with us. I wrapped both my arms around her shoulders. She draped her arms over mine and we sat in silence for a long time.

I was finally home.